HER ALIEN MASTERS

CAPTIVES OF PRA'KIR, BOOK 3

RENEE ROSE

Published in the United States of America

Renee Rose Romance

Editor:

Kate Richards, Wizards in Publishing

This e-book is a work of fiction. While reference might be made to actual historical events or existing locations, the names, characters, places and incidents are either the product of the authors' imaginations or are used fictitiously, and any resemblance to actual persons, living or dead, business establishments, events, or locales is entirely coincidental.

This book contains descriptions of many BDSM and sexual practices, but this is a work of fiction and, as such, should not be used in any way as a guide. The author and publisher will not be responsible for any loss, harm, injury, or death resulting from use of the information contained within. In other words, don't try this at home, folks!

❀ Created with Vellum

CONTENTS

1

The Council of Nine reported today that in lieu of death sentences for the five female aliens whose ship crashed on the freeway, killing innocent Pra'kirians, the aliens will be fostered out for conditioning to society. Sources say the aliens, who came from a planet called Earth, may have been hit by debris circling our planet, which caused them to crash and their fuel cell to explode. According to military sources, there is no possibility for the aliens to communicate with their planet or ever return. The information on where each alien will be placed will be kept confidential.

— Pra'kirian News Report

~.~

ALL JAKK WANTED WAS a moment of peace and quiet. Too bad they no longer existed in his world. He left the busy courtroom and entered his office, head pounding.

"Judge Ereen, your brother left an urgent message. I think it's about your nieces."

He barely contained a groan. Again? Really? "Thank you, Sanda."

She nodded and looked quickly away—a reaction he got from most females. Make that all females. Born with eyes two different colors, he was a misfit in Pra'kirian society.

He flicked on his communicator, which had been silenced while he held court. "Call Gav'n."

The screen sprang open, showing Gav'n's face. The furrow between his twin brother's brows was deeper than usual, and he appeared to be out of breath.

"What happened now?"

Gav'n's head bobbed like he was jogging, and sweat beaded at his forehead. "The nanny left them—alone. According to Darley, their rashes got worse, and the nanny panicked. I *told* the stupid woman they weren't contagious. Anyway, the girls are without supervision at the moment, and I can't go home because we're in the middle of a smuggling raid."

Pain throbbed in Jakk's temples. He'd had the same headache since the day the aliens' ship crashed and killed their sister, leaving him and his twin brother responsible for their three young nieces. He'd gone from living a quiet life alone to attempting to coexist with Gav'n and their nieces in his sister's home. To say it wasn't going well was an understatement.

He muttered a curse. "I'll go. The magistrate is going to have my ass over all these absences, though."

This was the fifth nanny they'd lost since taking custody of the girls. Between the children's unexplained skin rash—blisters that came and went all over their bodies—and their general bad behavior, it had become impossible to find anyone willing to stay with them. *Dammit.* He should have Gav'n arrest today's nanny for leaving her post. Endangerment of underage children was a serious offense on Pra'kir.

"Thanks. I'll see you at home when I'm off," Gav'n said, already focusing away from the screen on whatever he was hunting. The screen blipped off.

Jakk sighed. He'd better explain the situation to the magistrate in person. Even though he held a position of power and technically could come and go as he pleased, he'd been absent more than he'd been in the courthouse lately, and with Rowth, it was better to communicate any problems than have him find them on his own.

"I'm out for the day," he told Sanda as he left his office. He ignored her curious gaze. "I'll visit the magistrate in person on my way out. Please contact me on the communicator with anything important."

"Yes, Your Honor."

He took the chute to the second to top floor to see his boss, Rowth Lashat, the general magistrate for the superior court and the highest authority on the planet, except for the Council of Nine.

Rowth's assistant sat in reception, tapping away on her screen. "Is the magistrate in?"

The receptionist lifted her head. "Yes, Your Honor. Is he expecting you?"

"No. I only need a minute, though."

"Judge Endove to see you, Your Honor," she said into the communication device. She glanced back up at Jakk. "You may go in."

He opened the door and stepped inside but didn't take a seat. He didn't have time for a long conversation—his young nieces were completely unsupervised at the moment. "I have to leave for the day —again."

Setting his tablet aside, the magistrate raised his eyebrows in a rare show of emotion.

"I know. I don't find it acceptable, either, but Gav'n and I are having a terrible time keeping a nanny to watch our nieces. They can't go to school, either, due to some health issues. Needless to say, I understand this is a problem, and we're working on a long-term solution."

Rowth stood and walked around his desk, then perched on the edge of it. "I may have a solution for you, Jakk."

Doubtful. "Oh?" He did his best to appear polite.

"The Council of Nine has ruled the aliens are to be fostered out."

"I'd heard that," he said neutrally. And? How could this possibly apply to him?

"They were responsible for your sister's death. Doesn't it seem reasonable for one of them to give back to society by taking her place in your home and raising her children?"

Only years of presiding over court kept his jaw from dropping.

"With all due respect, my brother and I can hardly manage the raising of our nieces. We certainly couldn't foster another being."

"She will require obedience training, yes, but even though the aliens are young in Pra'kirian years, I believe they are full-grown adults—intelligent and capable of giving back to society, if we can find the right placement for them. Your brother's military police background and yours as a judge should make training her a simple matter—it's one of the reasons I'm considering your household. And once she's trained, you would have a servant for life. You might consider it an upfront investment. "

Jakk pushed on his right temple. "Is it even safe? To have one near children?"

Rowth searched for something on his communication pad and handed it to Jakk. "This is the file of the human I suggest you foster—Mirella Janison. She's a mechanical engineer who has shown protective behavior over the other humans. I believe the same instincts would translate to children of another species."

He stared at the photo. *"Oh."*

"Yes." Rowth's tone was generally dry, but even more so now, probably because the cold bastard guessed exactly what he was thinking.

The human was *stunning.* Small, yes—but fully developed. She had long, silky blonde hair—a color that had become increasingly rare with the homogenization on Pra'kir. Her large, wide-set eyes were sea green and, coupled with her bow-shaped mouth, gave her heart-stopping beauty. If she were Pra'kirian, she'd be guaranteed a career as a high-paid model or newscaster.

His heart thudded a little harder. Was Rowth suggesting her for them because Jakk had no chance of ever finding a mate with his mismatched eyes? While his superior was not the warm and fuzzy type, he could be thoughtful. Or pragmatic. Perhaps it suited Rowth to have this female situated with him.

He forced his gaze away from the enchanting photo of the female and back to Rowth. "So you're suggesting we train her as our nanny? And keep her...indefinitely?"

Yes, Rowth's shrewd gaze said he knew exactly what Jakk wanted to do with the little human. "That's correct. Unless the placement doesn't suit you, in which case, the Council would find another placement for her."

"I'd have to speak to Gav'n. Although"—he glanced back at the likeness—"I can't see he'd object, once he sees her. Will you send me this file?"

"Yes." A tiny curve quirked Rowth's lips. "Let me know as soon as possible, and I will present the suggested placement to the Council of Nine," he said, referring to the true governing body of their planet. Rowth stood from his perch on the desk. "I'll expect you tomorrow."

"Yes, Your Honor." He left the government building and jumped in his shuttle before calling Gav'n up on the screen. "I'm heading home, now."

"Did he give you a hard time?"

"The general magistrate? No. Actually, he suggested a solution. He'd like to put our names in for consideration to foster one of the aliens who crashed their ship onto the freeway. He seems to believe she should repay her debt to our family by taking Analie's place as a permanent nanny to the kids."

Gav'n's lip curled. "What do you think about that idea?"

His cock thickened imagining what it would mean to, essentially, *own* a female—a gorgeous female, no less, who would have no choice but to live with an undesirable male. To have one living in their house, obedient to their commands, subservient to their rules, subject to their punishments.... The idea inflamed him.

While he wasn't entirely inexperienced with women, the only sexual encounters he'd had were threesomes with his brother. With his genetic deformity, he couldn't attract any female on his own, so Gav'n brought them in and shared. It worked for casual sex, but no female would stay with them—scratch that—with *him*, permanently. And he had a feeling Gav'n was reluctant to take a permanent mate when Jakk couldn't.

"Well, she'd require obedience training. But look." With one hand maneuvering the shuttle along the track, he used the other to forward the file Rowth had sent. A beep from Gav'n's communicator confirmed he'd received it.

"Whoa."

"I know."

"They didn't look so pretty on the clip of their crash the news keeps playing. Is that really her? I say *hell, yes*. I'll bring the little female to heel with a firm hand and a *lot* of love."

"I'll tell the general magistrate." He zipped into the back alley behind their sister's townhouse and parked. "I'm home now. Hopefully the girls haven't set fire to their bedroom by now."

"Good luck."

He disconnected the video feed and parked in the allotted space for his shuttle.

Now, to deal with his young nieces. One rebellious human female had to be a walk on the beach compared to them.

2

Mira paced in the confines of her prison quarters. She, Blythe, Sarai and Lily had been placed in separate cells since their sentencing and other than the photo the magistrate had flashed them, she had yet to see their fifth shipmate, Brinley, who'd required serious medical care following their crash on Pra'kir.

Apparently, after their fuel cell exploded off the beach of Endermere, they'd been tried for the murder of the citizens killed by their ship. They hadn't been invited to their trial, but the result was they'd be fostered out to Pra'kirian families rather than being put to death.

So, yeah. The guards thought they ought to be kissing feet in gratitude, but she'd withhold any celebrations for when she saw how this all panned out. All she knew was any return to Earth would be technologically impossible, so her fate lay with the Pra'kirians.

A door clanged open down the hall. "Judge Ereen and Police Commissioner Ereen, coming through!" Every important person was announced this way when they entered. Heavy footsteps of more than one being drew closer. Two enormous males stopped at her cell, accompanied by the asshole guard. The men looked alike—they must be twins, although one had mismatched eyes—one green, one brown. He stood slightly taller and had close-cropped brown hair, while the other had brown eyes slightly shaggier hair of the same color. Both were over seven feet tall, with broad shoulders and muscular definition that showed through their clothing.

The brown-eyed man casually leaned against the bars and grinned at her. Not a leer—a genuine smile, though a bit roguish. The first friendly face she'd seen on Pra'kir since they arrived. "Hey, little alien."

Her pulse sped up. He was also the best-looking male she'd seen, on Earth or Pra'kir. And his brother wasn't hard on the eyes, either.

She didn't answer, waiting to see what they wanted.

He turned to the guard. "Does she talk? Does her translator work?" The doctors had injected her with some sort of serum enabling her to speak and understand their language.

The guard ran his stick along the bars, making a clanging loud enough to split her head. "Oh, she talks, but sometimes it takes the proper persuasion."

The slightly taller, more serious brother frowned. "I hope, for your sake, she's been well treated."

Surprise flitted over the guard's face, as if he hadn't expected rebuke. "Of course she has."

Lying fuck.

"Has he mistreated you?" the friendly brother asked.

She narrowed her eyes at the guard but still didn't think it wise to answer.

The taller man, who had a forbidding manner, tapped the lock. "Open it."

The guard unfastened the lock and swung the door wide to allow both men to enter. If they had been human, she would have placed them in their mid-thirties. They held themselves with confidence—although in totally different ways. The taller one had a stiff, formal manner, while the other exhibited a casual, devil-may-care grace.

Mismatched Eyes cleared his throat. "Mirella? I'm Jakk. This is my brother Gav'n. We're your new guardians. We're responsible for conditioning you to fit in with Pra'kirian society."

"Mira."

Jakk raised his brows. He didn't appear mean, but he certainly had "stern" down to a T.

"I go by Mira, for short."

Gav'n stepped closer, sauntering around her. She turned so she wouldn't have her back to him, but he put a large hand on her shoulder to hold her still then picked up her wrists, bound with anesthetic child restraints borrowed from the local hospital because her wrists were too small for their handcuffs. Essentially, zipties. His fingers were warm, touch gentle.

"These are too tight on her." Did he actually sound angry?

"Believe me, Commissioner, you don't want to take those off her," the guard spoke up. "She may be small and female, but she fights like a wild animal. All the aliens do."

"I'll take my chances," Gav'n said mildly. He withdrew a small penknife from his pocket and cut off the zip ties.

She sucked in her breath as blood rushed back into her arms, sending pinpricks of pain to her hands. The large male turned her to face him then rubbed the deep red indentations on her wrists. Her eyes found his in shock. She stood frozen, trapped in his intense chocolate-brown gaze while her insides fluttered and dropped.

"Female," he muttered, sounding awed, "You are even more beautiful than I expected."

She tried to pull her wrists away from him, more out of surprise at his words than fear or offense. *Beautiful* wasn't a word she'd choose to describe herself. Her older sisters were beautiful, and perfect in every other way. She'd always been the plain tomboy who couldn't get anything right.

The hulking male held her fast, continuing with the firm stroking of his thumbs over her pulses. "Easy, little alien. You're safe now. We're taking you home with us."

She noticed the urge to snort came and left without moving her to actual sound. Oddly, she did find the men—were they called men here?—comforting.

Gav'n twisted her wrists behind her back again and held them loosely caged in his larger hand. "Let's go, pretty girl." He propelled her forward, out of the cell and past his brother, whose intense gaze confused her. It was so different from the curiosity, fear, or animosity they'd received from most of the other Pra'kirians they'd seen since they arrived. Like the general magistrate, this man wasn't afraid, but his expression wasn't one of cool indifference, either. It was more...proprietary. And she sensed an excitement behind it, which ought to make her nervous, but instead had her...*intrigued.*

"I understand punishments are necessary, but if we find out from the girl you've mistreated her, there will be consequences," he clipped to the guard.

If the way the guard paled was any indication, Jakk had the authority to back his promise up. Was he the judge or the police commissioner? Judge, she'd guess. Yeah, he probably had the authority to do a great many things.

She'd already learned through experience the Pra'kirians had a penchant for corporal punishment. Would this one enjoy wielding a strap as much as her prison guard had? The thought shouldn't send a shiver of excitement down her spine, but it did.

Gav'n must have noticed. "Don't worry. My brother may seem scary, but he likes feisty alien females as much as I do." He propelled her down the hall, and Jakk fell in beside her. She dared glance up at Jakk—actually, she had to crane her neck to see him. He seemed more formidable up close. His resting face was stern. No smile lines crinkled around his eyes or mouth, the way they did on his brother, and the mismatched eyes gave him an even more alien appearance to her.

Who were these males, and what would they do with her? Another shiver ran down her spine.

"Are you cold, little alien?" Gav'n asked.

"Human," she corrected. Not *alien.*

He flicked his eyebrows and shot a quick glance over her head to his brother. "Human, yes. We'll discuss the proper way to respond to a question when we get home."

Proper way to respond to a question? Fuck that. If they thought they'd be teaching her manners, they could jump off a cliff.

They led her out of the building to an underground parking garage of sorts. No—more like a train station, but with individual shuttles. They had no wheels, but instead, were attached to tracks. The brothers' shuttle was a metallic sky blue, shaped like a bullet.

A trio of males passed by and gawked openly at her.

Jakk unlocked the vehicle and opened the passenger door. "You'd better put her in manacles for the ride," he said to Gav'n. "She might try to escape."

Gav'n switched his grip, pulling her wrists together in front of her, instead of behind her back. "Actually," he said with a grin, "I think I'll hold onto her." He adjusted the huge bucket seat backward and sat in it, pulling her onto his lap. "If you try to get away, little alien—human —I will bare your little bottom and spank you until you are very sore and sorry. Right here, in public. Understand?"

She turned away to hide the flush flooding her face. *Spank* her? The guard had whipped her when she refused to eat. Now this male suggested spanking her like a child. Clearly, this species had a love affair with using the buttocks for punishment.

Without her permission, her awareness crept to her ass, which happened to be pressed tight against the huge alien's lap. Was that his cock? Oh Lord. Yep, his cock twitched under her.

Heat snaked between her legs, filling her core and bringing a buzzing to her clit. Under the scratchy yellow prison garb, her nipples hardened.

Gav'n gripped her jaw and turned her head toward him as Jakk climbed into the driver's seat. "*Yes, master,* is the only correct answer to that question."

So this was the conditioning they'd mentioned. She pressed her teeth together mutinously and willed the thrum between her legs to subside. She absolutely did not find any of this sexy.

Jakk settled in his seat and studied her with a cool gaze. "We're not the enemy, Mira. I promise."

Something about his use of her preferred name made the words ring with truth. It was probably some conditioning technique, though.

She opened her mouth but could think of no response, other than —*if you spank me, I'll cut off your balls.* Did the aliens even have balls? Lord, now she was thinking about their cocks again—yes, cocks plural. Because two very large male aliens were looking at her as if they owned her. Which, according to Pra'kirian law, they technically did.

Lord help her.

"We'll have a few days to settle in together and straighten out roles and expectations before the girls come home from our parents' house in the country." Jakk maneuvered the shuttle forward and accelerated, entering a rapid stream of traffic.

She stiffened. "Girls?"

He glanced over with those quirky, mismatched eyes. She wondered if the trait was common on Pra'kir. "Weren't you told about your placement?"

"No."

He turned wooden. She wrestled with Gav'n to get her hands free, only because she desperately wanted to clutch at the dashboard or find a handle somewhere as the bullet shuttle zoomed past several other shuttles, passing them on the right.

"You are to give back to the society you've taken from. Our sister was killed by your ship's crash. Gav'n and I were left guardianship of her children, our three young nieces. Your duty will be their care."

A chill seeped into her chest and sank like a stone, closely followed by panic. The urge to cry and throw herself out of the vehicle also came simultaneously. She had never contemplated what it would be like to come face to face with a relative of someone they'd killed. And now they expected her to *raise the children* of a victim? Those kids would hate her. How could they not? And she'd feel guilty and horrible for the rest of her life—assuming she stayed with them for the rest of her life, which was a distinct possibility, since without their fuel cell, there'd be no way to communicate with Earth or ever get a ship off Pra'kir. If their ship hadn't crashed, they could have used the star charts to figure out where they were, because the ship had the coordinates of where they'd come from. But the stars on Pra'kir had different names, and none of the constellations were recognizable.

"I—" She cleared her throat, still struggling with Gav'n for the use of her hands. "I'm sorry for your loss. Crashing here was out of our control, and we never intended to injure any beings."

"So you say." Gav'n wrapped a muscled arm around her waist and squeezed her against him. His cock had definitely grown with her struggles and now pressed insistently against her ass.

She blinked back tears. "I can't see how this is a good idea. Your nieces—they must be grieving terribly. Having me around will only amplify their pain."

The males exchanged an incomprehensible glance.

"They're grieving, regardless," Gav'n said. "I don't think you can make it much worse."

Oh hell. What did that mean?

"Hey." Gav'n swapped hands again, moving the one at her waist to grip her throat. She jerked with alarm, but his fingers didn't tighten. Instead, he used the palm at her throat to pull her head backward until it rested on his shoulder in an arch. "You're responsible for our situation, and we need your help."

Well, damn. It was about as compelling an argument as she could expect. After being treated as Public Enemy Number One by everyone else, they hit her where it hurt by appealing to her humanity. Humanity—hah. They weren't human. Well, her sense of compassion, then. Her heart.

Motherless children and two hot alien guardians who needed her help. *Damn.* They were difficult to harden herself against.

She sighed and relaxed into Gav'n's hold, watching the scenery flash by. Endermere, the coastal city where they'd crashed, was built upon a C-shaped section of peninsula. It appeared green and lush, with little pollution and lots of vegetation for such a densely populated area.

She braced when Jakk passed another shuttle at an insane speed.

There was no brake pedal she could see. The controls mainly seemed to consist of a joystick.

Jakk must have noticed her watching because his eyes slid over to hers. "You're an engineer, right?"

She nodded.

"Did you fly the craft that crashed here?"

"I maintained and repaired it."

"Then driving one of these should be easy for you. Everything's controlled with this." He patted the joystick.

"How do you brake?"

Jakk's brow furrowed. "Break what?"

Stupid translator. "Slow down. How do you slow down?"

He tapped the joystick again until she looked at it, then he pushed the entire stick down. The shuttle slowed.

"Ah. Clever." Her jaw dropped as they sped along a cliff's edge, standing high above a sparkling turquoise bay. Pra'kir was unbelievably beautiful—a fact she hadn't had time to note when they'd crashed and had to run for their lives while the locals had attacked. It was like Earth in many ways, with blue skies, mountains, and oceans.

"We'll teach you to drive after your initial conditioning," Gav'n promised. "Our sister's shuttle has automatic steering, so we can program a destination in, but I have a feeling you're the type who likes to understand how things work."

"What exactly is this conditioning?"

Jakk made a sudden turn, screeching around a bend in the tracks to shoot off toward a cluster of tightly packed multi-story buildings, nested along the coast.

She stifled a squeal when the shuttle dived down off the tracks, swerved around several slower shuttles, and zipped into a tiny garage accessed from a narrow alleyway at the rear of the row of buildings. He parked next to two other bullet shuttles in a miniscule yard. Well, more like a small garden with flowers and plants making neat rows along the back and one side of the parking spaces.

"We'll talk about it when we get inside," Jakk said.

She didn't like the sound of that.

~.~

GAV'N LED their little human up the back steps of his sister's home, which was situated above a bakery in a tight row of historic waterfront buildings. The place was small, but he and Jakk had decided uprooting the children from their home would be too stressful for them following the death of their mother, so they'd moved in, the two of them sharing what had been Analie's bedroom.

"The girls are at our parents' house for a few days, while we get you settled in." *And make sure you aren't a danger.* He hoped they got her settled quickly because their elderly parents couldn't take the stress of caring for the girls, especially when they were still grieving their Analie's death, too.

From the concern Mira had shown over the girls' feelings, he thought this would work. They just had to convince their little ward of it.

"Clothes off," he said, releasing her wrists. She still wore one of the bright yellow prison jumpersuits normally worn by juvenile offenders, since the adult uniforms were too large.

She spun to face him, mouth agape. "Excuse me?"

"You heard me. Take off your prison uniform. For the initial conditioning, we'll need you naked at all times. It enhances your sense of vulnerability and submission and helps establish our roles as your masters."

"Fuck. That."

He didn't understand the command to *fuck that.* Not only was she not being specific about what he was supposed to have casual relations with, but the only thing he was in a mood to fuck was her. Unfortunately, it appeared more like she wanted to kick his teeth out, which was damn cute.

Jakk closed in from the other direction. "If we have to help you undress, Mira, you will earn your first consequence."

She bolted.

The little human ran straight for the door, moving faster than he would've expected. Jakk lunged forward, catching her around the waist, covering her mouth when she screamed. He carried her a few steps forward, offering her up for Gav'n to undress. She didn't make it easy, wriggling and twisting like a wild animal, but he managed to work the prison suit off her while his brother held her flailing body.

"And now your consequence." Jakk used an emotionless tone, as if they always stripped young females and paddled their naked bottoms. His brother carried her to the settee, and Gav'n followed, sitting next to Jakk, so Mira's head fell in his lap when her bottom went over Jakk's. He took control of Mira's wrists while Jakk scissored one thigh over her kicking legs.

Mira opened her mouth as if to bite him, but his reflexes were quicker, and he caught her by the hair and pulled her face away in time. "Ah ah, little human. Biting will earn you a second consequence."

Jakk's palm landed on her bare ass with a resounding crack, and the little thing jerked. Gav'n watched as first shock, then fury scrawled across her features. The pink imprint of Jakk's large hand bloomed on one of her cheeks. Jakk slapped her again, harder, on the other side. Jakk picked up the pace, spanking her rapidly on one cheek then the other, right where she sat.

"Ow! What is this? You can't keep me here like this—*ow*!"

Her resistance turned him on. Still holding her by the wrists and the hair, Gav'n leaned forward and spoke softly in her ear, making his voice as loving and gentle as he knew how. "Easy, Mira. It's a spanking. To teach you to obey. That's all."

Her eyes swiveled to peer at him as best as they could with his hair-hold. They revealed betrayal. Her small, rounded breasts heaved as she panted with the pain and stress.

He shoved a pillow between her head and his lap and released her hair, massaging her scalp when her head fell to the pillow. To his satisfaction, she remained collapsed, as if she'd accepted her fate. He continued to massage her head while Jakk slapped away at her rapidly reddening ass.

And a rather perfect ass it was. As was the rest of her. Pale ivory skin glowed with health; her slender body was built of lean muscle, legs long. She was certainly the most beautiful creature he'd ever had the good fortune to disrobe.

The pain must have set in, because Mira lifted her head again, tugging against his hold on her wrists and squirming. Of course, with the two of them holding her down, she wasn't going anywhere.

Jakk spanked her steadily for another full minute and then stopped, rubbing her pink buttocks. His mismatched eyes had darkened, and Gav'n knew his brother must be as aroused as he was. Jakk drew in a deep breath, his palm roving over Mira's punished ass in a caress, now. "Do you smell that, Gav'n?" he asked thickly.

Gav'n inhaled through his nose. *Feminine arousal.* The delicious scent of Mira's musk reached his nostrils. "I think Mira enjoyed her spanking as much as we liked giving it."

Her head flew up, anger blazing in her eyes.

He laughed. "Your body can't lie, little one."

Jakk released one of her legs from under his leg-hold, prying her thighs open to slide two fingers along her sex. He held up the glistening proof for both Gav'n and Mira to see.

Mira's face flushed, and she struggled with renewed vigor. Jakk slapped her ass a few more times, and she subsided, panting prettily.

"There's no reason to be upset. You see, we haven't explained this part yet. We will give out punishments—as often as you need them or we see fit—but we will also give you pleasure."

Jakk stroked his fingers over her delicate slit again with a sensuous glide, up and down with three long strokes.

Mira let out a shaky breath when Jakk stopped.

"Would you like us to show you pleasure?"

She sucked her lower lip into her mouth and shook her head, but he didn't believe her. Her eyes didn't meet his gaze, didn't have the fire burning there he'd seen a moment before.

Jakk returned his fingers to her sex, and this time she arched, lifting her ass toward him for more. Jakk grinned.

"No?" he prodded when Jakk had once more removed his fingers. "Are you sure? My brother and I are very good at giving a female everything she could ever desire, and more. Have you ever had two males at once, Mira?"

She shook her head and let out a whimper, which he thought might be her concession they'd won.

"All you have to say is, *yes, master.*"

The fury that had been absent flared in her expression, but Jakk had already returned his fingers to her clit, and whatever he was doing made Mira suck in her breath with a sharp inhalation and buck on Jakk's lap.

"Say it. Yes, master."

"Fuck you."

Again, based on the blaze in her eyes, he didn't think she truly meant she wanted to have intercourse. Later, he'd ask her about the translation.

Jakk freed her other leg from under his thigh. "Flip her over." In tandem, they rolled her in the air to lie on their laps on her back.

"What are you—?" She lifted her head and watched as Jakk eased one of her knees up toward her shoulder and lowered his mouth to her sex.

He licked along her slit, parting her nether lips with his tongue, stroking inside with short licks. "She tastes delicious." He sat up.

"*Yes, master.* Do you want Jakk to continue?"

For one moment, Gav'n thought she was going to cry. Her lips trembled, and she blinked a few times. "Yes, master." Her defeat caused her anguish, but the moment Jakk lowered his head, gripping her lifted thigh and applying his tongue with alacrity, her head dropped back, eyes rolling.

Her rasping breath made him harder than a rock. Gods of Na, he wanted to pick her up and sit her right down on his stiffened cock, make her ride it until they both came, screaming loud enough for every customer in the bakery downstairs to hear. But he and Jakk had discussed the parameters of Mira's conditioning before they'd picked her up, and they'd decided no intercourse unless she specifically desired it. Otherwise, they were taking advantage of their position as her guardians. They both held important offices with the government, and if it ever got back to the council they'd excessively abused their ward in any way—went beyond normal punishments and rewards—they might be disgraced.

Still wrestling with her wrists in one hand, he gripped her jaw with the other, turning her face toward him to watch it contort with pleasure. He plunged his thumb into her mouth, and she immediately sucked it, hard. Ah...hell, yes. He imagined it was his cock between her lush lips, his cock her tongue stroked and cheeks hollowed to suck.

Jakk shoved two fingers inside her, and she cried out, her animalistic sound bringing Gav'n close to the edge of control. Jakk pumped in and out of her while flicking her clit with his tongue, and she made an incoherent sound and convulsed, her beautiful breasts lifting up off his lap, head falling back.

So beautiful. He released her wrists and took his thumb out of her mouth, wanting to stroke her soft little body, to praise and reward her for the trust she'd shown in giving herself over to them. He cupped her small breasts, stroked one palm down her side, burrowed another in her hair.

"Beautiful girl," he murmured. "Does that feel better? Your masters will always take care of you."

Her eyes blinked open and found his, searching. For what? He didn't know.

He cradled her face and lowered his head, brushing her lips with his. They were impossibly soft and small, like the rest of her. She didn't kiss him back, so he gave her space. In time, they'd win her affection. At least, he hoped so.

But then, he was still hoping it would prove true with their nieces, too.

~.~

JAKK ALLOWED his twin to lift Mira up to sit on his lap, where Gav'n cupped her breasts and stroked her skin.

With her taste still on his tongue, he could hardly deny his brother his fill of her lush little body. He stood and adjusted his throbbing cock in his pants. He needed to do something to distract himself, or he'd take advantage of her new trust in every way possible.

"Are you hungry, *pashika*?" He cupped her chin to gaze into her dazed face.

She blinked and stared back at him. Funny how she didn't flinch and look away like other females did, even after directly focusing on his eyes. "What's *pashika*?"

His lips quirked. He hadn't thought about the endearment when he spoke it, but, of course, it wouldn't translate. "It's a bird found here on Pra'kir. A little bird. We use it as a term of affection."

Her cheeks turned a pretty shade of pink. "I'm not sure I understand...any of this."

"It's simple, really. We're a family, now." He spoke the words before censoring himself. And as soon as they left his mouth, he kicked himself for showing his hand so soon. His deepest desire. He wanted this situation to work, not only for the girl's sake, but because it was his only chance at having a family.

Well, that wasn't true. He, Gav'n, and the girls were making a family of sorts, or they were trying. But he'd never have a female of his own. The best he'd ever hoped for was to share Gav'n's future mate, on occasion, but even that seemed doubtful. Once his brother was mated, they'd have their own children, and including him wouldn't be a part of their plan.

~.~

MIRA'S BODY still trembled from both the spanking and the orgasm afterward. Her heated ass tingled, the memory of Jakk's powerful hand still as real as Gav'n's large palms that now stroked up and down her body. She sat—sprawled, really—over his lap, head falling back against his shoulder, legs parted wide and dangling over his knees.

The languid relaxation from her orgasm had ebbed, though, with Jakk's mention of food. So far, her digestive system hadn't adjusted to Pra'kirian food. In prison, the guard had whipped her and force-fed her every time she refused to eat, but, fortunately, she'd convinced him, due to her size, she required far less food than was actually true. She actually didn't want to ingest any more of the bellyache-inducing spicy glop they served her.

Jakk had gone to the kitchen for food. Gav'n stroked up her inner thigh, slowing as he reached the apex.

Her trembling increased. She fought her body's urge to thrust her pelvis forward, toward those thick fingers. God, Jakk's finger-fucking had been amazing. Because, yeah, his digits were almost the size of a human male's cock. Lord, how big must their cocks be?

She shook her head. She had to stop thinking of them that way. These men had set her so off-kilter, she didn't know her head from her still-throbbing and heated tail. She shouldn't have enjoyed that punishment so much. It was so vastly different from the guard's whippings. The spanking had been intimate, over their laps, and there'd been two of them holding her down. No, that wasn't what made it different. Their intent had. The guard wanted to hurt her, he'd enjoyed it. Well, these two might have enjoyed it, too. *So what in the hell was so different?*

The affection.

They acted like they adored her. Even when she fought them.

Okay, that was pretty hot. Why it turned her on so much, she couldn't be sure. She certainly hadn't ever had giant alien rape fantasies. But, yeah...their domination appealed to her a helluva lot more than the guard's had.

Which didn't mean she could let her defenses down. She still didn't truly understand this arrangement. She was going to be their...what? Slave? Housewife? Sex toy?

Why did all three spark a coil of desire in her core?

Gav'n's fingers arrived at her sex and lightly brushed her outer lips. She bit back a moan. His cock flexed against her ass. He lowered his lips to her ear. "Little girl, whenever you want your masters' cocks, you let us know."

She froze. Did she have a choice?

Did she really want one? She sure as hell wasn't going to beg again. The first time had been humiliating enough.

Jakk returned with a plate heaped with food. He pulled up a chair and sat in front of her.

She stiffened.

Gav'n hitched her higher on his lap. "What's the matter, *pashika*? Are you scared of Jakk because he punished you?"

She didn't answer.

He gripped her jaw and turned her face in his direction. "When I ask you a question, I expect an answer, delivered in a respectful manner. *Yes, Master* or *no, Master*. Understand?"

She tried to wrench her face from his hold.

"Do you need another spanking?"

She wanted to keep fighting, but better sense prevailed. "No." Although she couldn't entirely see his face from her position, she sensed his glower. "No, *Master*."

Oddly, his scowl produced an uptick in her heart rate. Did she actually care what he thought of her? She supposed it made sense—these two were the first Pra'kirians to show her any kindness. She probably should think twice about pissing them off. Her still-stinging bottom crawled as she sensed the threat of more punishment.

"No, Master," she muttered.

He released her face. Jakk sat with the plate of food balanced on his knees. He stabbed a sliced bit of either a fruit or vegetable, bright-red in color, with a two-pronged fork, and held it to her lips.

She closed her mouth and turned away. "I'm not hungry...Master."

Gav'n immediately resumed his stroking of her leg, presumably rewarding her for calling Jakk *Master*.

And damn if the simple gesture didn't make her wet.

Jakk's eyebrows lifted. "No?" Skepticism scrawled across his face. "You're thin, *pashika*. If I find out those guards withheld your food in prison—"

"They didn't withhold food," she mumbled. "They force-fed me."

Jakk lowered his fork, his expression inscrutable. "Why? Did you refuse to eat?"

"We don't eat the same amount as you—did that ever occur to you tyrannical giants? And our bodies aren't used to your food. How do you think you'd feel to be stuffed full of some other planet's spicy food?"

Jakk lowered his fork. "Another punishment for tone," he said to his brother.

"Yes." Gav'n abruptly lifted her from his lap and flipped her face down, her head the opposite direction it had been for her first spanking. He pinned both her hands at the small of her back and threw one leg over her closest thigh. She struggled, more out of principle than any belief she might get free.

"I'll get the plug. It might help her remember to speak respectfully."

The plug. She searched her brain for any reference but couldn't figure out how a plug could be a spanking implement. Taking advantage of her one free leg, she kicked it in the vain hope she might strike her captor.

He leaned over and spoke in her ear. "You kick me with that foot, *pashika*, and I'll make you one very sorry little girl."

Her pussy and anus both clenched at his words in some weird, reflexive reaction to his dominance. If she was totally honest with herself, she'd admit he'd scared her. His tone hadn't sounded teasing this time, and she had a feeling he meant business. Whatever it meant to be *one sorry little girl*, she didn't want to find out.

Jakk's heavy footsteps signaled his return. She sensed him

standing over her, and then his large hands prized her butt cheeks apart.

She squealed and attempted to tighten them, her bottom hole twitching, but a heavy slap on the back of her thigh made her howl and lose focus. A hard, cool object pushed against her back entrance.

A *plug!* Duh. Dear Lord—these Pra'kirians truly were perverted sadists, weren't they?

She fought hard, fought for all she was worth, wriggling and squirming, trying to get away, but she only succeeded in getting her ass soundly toasted—by Gav'n, she thought. Of course, as soon as he stopped spanking her, one of them pried her cheeks apart, and the plug returned.

"No," she whimpered. Tears of anger burned in the corners of her eyes.

"Hush, little girl. You were naughty. I asked you to speak to us respectfully, and you failed. This will help you remember who is in charge of you." That came from Gav'n. Jakk had said very little, but he seemed to be the one who inserted the oiled object into her ass.

"Stop," she pleaded, arching up, trying to squeeze her bottom closed.

"Look at me." Yes, all the playfulness was gone from Gav'n's voice.

Against her will, she turned to glare at him.

He met her gaze evenly. "It only hurts if you fight it. Lie back down, open your ass, and take the punishment your masters have decided is appropriate."

A stupid tear leaked out of her eye, which seriously pissed her off. She didn't want them to see her break.

He held her eyes, the command she'd heard in his voice equally evident in his expectant expression.

"I hate you," she mumbled as she collapsed over his thighs, willing her sphincter to relax. He probably was right—it would only hurt if she fought it.

"I hope that's not true, *pashika*. Because we definitely don't hate you." Now Gav'n's voice became a caress.

She held her breath as the plug breached her hole. Hummed her protest when it stretched her tight opening wider and wider. Screeched when she was certain it wouldn't fit, right before it sank into her then lodged in place.

"It's in, Mira. We'll take it out when you've demonstrated respect for our authority." Jakk's chair scraped. "Sit up and look at me."

Gav'n lifted her back onto his lap, facing his brother. Straddling Gav'n's knees had the effect of presenting her pussy to Jakk and suspending her freshly spanked, burning, and plugged ass between Gav'n's thighs.

Aaaaand her nipples beaded up. This shouldn't be sexy to her. Why in the fuck was she responding to this treatment? Oh, maybe because it was ubersexual. Was this really the way they dealt with prisoners on Pra'kir? Or was it special, for her, as a young female?

Jakk cupped her chin, stroking his thumb along her cheek. "So the food bothers your stomach, little one?"

Relief he'd actually listened to her brought fresh tears to her eyes. She blinked angrily, trying to pull her face away from his grip.

"Prison food is nourishing—at least to our species—but not particularly fresh. Try a little of the things I prepared, and we'll see how you fare." He picked up the fork again and held it to her lips.

It was a reasonable request, and she had to admit the food on his plate did appear more appetizing than the hellishly spicy grains and gray meats from prison.

She waited a beat, only because her rebellious side had to assert itself, and then parted her lips.

The fruit had been salted—no—spiced. Both salted and spiced, it seemed, almost like the Latin American tradition of applying chili and lime to certain fruits. It was both unfamiliar and satisfying at once. She rolled the too-big bite around in her mouth, juice dribbling from her lips.

~.~

THEIR BEAUTIFUL HUMAN had Gav'n's cock so hard, he thought he'd burst. He watched her full, perfect lips move as she tried the bite of *madlyne* fruit Jakk had fed her. When a drip of juice ran down the corner of her mouth, he gripped her nape and caught it with his tongue.

She held still for him, her breath sucking in on a gasp.

He hadn't expected that. She'd fought the plug and spanking like a little demon. Maybe he was delusional, but he thought they were already getting through to her. They'd shown her a taste of both pleasure and pain. Soon, he hoped, they'd prove themselves worthy masters, and she'd accept her fate.

They'd only had her for a few short hours, but already he adored her. He loved everything about her. The intelligence behind those spectacular green-blue eyes, the fight she gave, and her beautiful surrender at moments like this one. She seemed so much more complex than a Pra'kirian female.

"What did you think?" He brushed his lips across the shell of her ear.

Wariness hooded her eyes, but she said in a hoarse voice. "I like it."

"I like it, *Master*. You're answering a question. Show respect."

Her shoulders sagged and, as much as they required her submission, he hated seeing her defeated. "I like it, Master." She sounded resentful, now.

Jakk fed her another bite, watching her mouth as intently as Gav'n had. Damn, he couldn't wait to have those supple lips around his cock. When she consented. As good hosts, he and Jakk preferred to go slow and win her over gently. However, providing for her sexual enjoyment was part of their duty. Just as it was her duty to accept or be punished. Soon, though. Soon, they'd win her submission and affection, and she'd willingly give all of herself.

"Okay, so the *madlyne* fruit seems fine," Jakk observed. "We will give it a few hours to be sure, and then introduce another food."

The fight left Mira's face. "Thank you...Master." The *Master* came as an afterthought, but he considered it a huge win.

Jakk fed her the rest of the *madlyne* on the plate, leaving the other foods he'd brought untouched. "Was it enough, Mira?"

She nodded, "Yes, Master....thank you."

Gav'n coasted his palms up her body and cupped her breasts, testing their weight, squeezing and kneading until she arched into his hands. "Good girl. You're doing so well, *pashika*. Thank you for using your manners." He rolled the nipple of one breast between his thumb and forefinger as his other hand stroked down her belly and over her trimmed mound.

She squirmed, as if to stop him, and he delivered a light slap to her pussy. "Hold still. Your master wants to reward you."

Jakk watched with glittering eyes. He leaned forward and brought his hand up between her legs, as well, reaching toward her suspended bottom, where he grabbed the butt plug.

Gav'n tapped her clit, and she rocked forward to meet his fingers. "I'll bet you'd like us to remove the plug now, wouldn't you?" he breathed in her ear.

Jakk slowly pumped the plug in and out of her ass, and she whimpered, pussy suddenly gushing her delectable arousal. "She likes that," he murmured.

She shook her head rapidly against his chest. "No...I don't." She sounded breathless.

Jakk repeated the plug pump while he circled her clit with his middle finger, loving the way the little nubbin had stiffened, engorged with blood.

"No," she whimpered, writhing, legs straightening and bending as she shifted her pelvis restlessly around.

"You mean, *yes*, little one. *Yes, Master.* Say it."

"No." Another moan.

"Do you need my digits again, *pashika*?" He'd never heard Jakk sound so affectionate. Usually, his brother was stiff or stoic with females.

Another rapid head shake, but her breath had turn to pants, cheeks glowing with excitement.

"I think she's lying, Jakk." He grinned at his brother and slapped her pussy three times.

She shrieked.

"We should punish her for lying."

Jakk grinned back. "Yes," he drawled. "After her reward, another punishment."

She tossed her head in confusion, her lovely straight blonde hair fanning out against his shirt.

Jakk screwed two fingers inside her while Gav'n continued to tease her clit. Jakk renewed his pumping of the butt plug, alternating the strokes. When his fingers delved deep, he pulled the butt plug out, stretching her wide. When he pulled his digits out, he pushed the plug back in.

Gav'n *tap tap tapped* her clit and squeezed her nipple.

Her moans took on a desperate pitch. "Please," she panted. "No...don't. Please....yes. Yes, Master—Masters—yes, please, oh God!" She screamed and threw her head back, lifting her pelvis from his lap.

Jakk shoved his fingers deep and kept them there, and this time he had the better view of her expressive face, twisting and contorting with her orgasm. It went on and on, with her mewling and bucking.

When it passed, all three of them went still. Mira sagged between his knees, panting.

Jakk eased his fingers out of her. "Stand up and bend over for your master. I'll take the plug out now."

He doubted she could have moved on her own, so he helped her stand, turned her to face him, and pulled her torso down until she hugged his waist with her arms, her ass presented high to his brother, head tucked against his side.

Jakk tugged on the plug, and she whimpered. "Relax, little one. Give me a long exhale." He stroked one hand up the graceful arch of her back, soothing her.

Gav'n felt her trembling, and he doubted her legs were doing their job holding her up. He, too, stroked her back. "Hum a little for me. Do you know what it means to hum?"

She obediently made a humming noise, affirming the translation worked.

Jakk nodded at him and slowly eased the plug free. "Good girl." He gave her ass a light slap and took the plug to the washroom to clean and disinfect it. When he returned, he said, "Let's give her a tour of the townhouse."

Gav'n lifted her to her feet and stood, then picked her up by the armpits and settled her legs around his waist, like a child.

The surprise on her face was priceless.

"Well, you're so small, *pashika*." He gave her ass a squeeze. "And your body is so delectable. It's natural for your master to want to carry you everywhere, especially when you're naked."

You can ride me, anytime, little human.

As if she guessed his lurid thought, she blushed, sliding her gaze away from his. Jakk led the tour, and he followed, carrying their new plaything.

"This house belonged to our sister," Jakk said as he walked toward the girls' room. "Her mate died of an incurable disease when Pritzi was just a baby—so he's been dead six years, now."

Mira's face grew sober. "What are their names and ages?" she asked hoarsely.

"Darley is the oldest. She's twenty-two. Jan is fourteen, and Pritzi is eight."

Mira's head twisted toward Jakk. "Twenty-two? Is she still considered a child? How old are you?"

"We're sixty-seven. According to your file, you're only twenty-nine but considered fully grown on Earth?" Jakk asked. "A twenty-nine-year-old is still in adolescence here."

"Our planet takes 365 days to rotate around the sun. What is it here?"

"Four hundred," Gav'n answered.

"How long is your average lifespan?"

"One hundred and sixty years."

She whistled. "So about twice ours."

His brother pushed open the door to the girls' room. "This is where they sleep."

Mira peered in at the three beds, her eyes running over every detail of the room as if they might quiz her on it later. "So they're eleven, seven and four in Earth years," she said softly. "Please tell me you'll let me wear clothes when they come."

Gav'n smirked. "If you behave." He winked.

"And we sleep upstairs." Jakk jogged up the flight of stair to the enormous master suite. Since the townhouse was a century-old building, wedged into Old Town, there were only the two bedrooms.

"We who?" Mira asked when he arrived at the top of the steps and set her on her feet to have a look around.

"It was Analie's. There are only two bedrooms, so Gav'n and I share it now. You'll sleep with us, and any punishments you earn will be delivered in private up here, after the girls come back from our parents."

"Where will I sleep?"

He hesitated. "In the bed with us. Unless you're naughty and we decide you don't deserve the bed, in which case, you'll sleep on a mat on the floor."

She rolled her eyes.

Jakk's hand snapped out and caught her chin. "Watch the eye-rolling, little human." Damn, his brother could look stern when he wanted to.

He didn't miss the shiver running through her. Good. She was already learning respect. Her lower jaw thrust forward. "So, am I your sex slave? Is that how Pra'kir deals with female convicts?"

Jakk winced ever so slightly and opened his mouth. Fearing his brother would tell her the truth—that they wouldn't have sex with her without her consent, Gav'n cut in. "No, *pashika*. Our role is to condition you. If you hope for sex, you'll have to earn it."

Her nostrils flared, whether with anger or interest, he couldn't be sure, but, a moment later, he scented her arousal, and a surge of victory pumped through him.

~.~

THE MASTER SUITE WAS BEAUTIFUL. As large as the entire downstairs, it had a sitting area with a couch, a giant canopy bed, and an en suite bathroom. The best feature, though, was the wall of floor-to-ceiling windows with a view of the bustling street and shops below, and, farther out, the sparkling bay.

She wondered if they'd take her to the bay. How normal would her life be here? Being nanny to their nieces made it seem like they'd be like an old-fashioned nuclear family. But, so far, nothing they'd done to her had been even close to conventional.

Being stripped naked, spanked, and pleasured repeatedly wasn't her idea of normal. And the worst part? She wasn't even sure she hated it. The way her clit still pulsed and her muscles had gone slack had her remembering every moment of their mastery.

Gawd—she'd never orgasmed like that in her life! What about these two giant males had her both entranced and fearful at the same time?

She walked to the windows, hiding her naked body behind the curtain to look out. "It's incredible," she murmured.

Gav'n stood behind her. He seemed to be the warm and cuddly one, Jakk, the stern disciplinarian. And skilled pleasure-giver.

Her clit throbbed again, remembering the way he'd worked the double-penetration on her like a fucking *pro*.

Not that she had much experience to judge. She'd had few boyfriends during her college training—one in the space program, but he'd turned out to be a two-timing ass. She'd never had two guys at once. Until today, she'd been an anal virgin.

In the few hours since the men had picked her up, she'd received more male attention than she had in the last three years put together. More attention, period. As the youngest, plainest, least-interesting child of a family of five superstars, she hadn't attracted much attention or praise. She'd joined the space program in an effort to prove she wasn't as boring and mediocre as her family had ascribed.

Now, she'd never see them again.

Oddly, she'd thought it would hurt more than it had. She missed her shipmates more than her family. Where had Brinley, Blythe, Sarai and Lily been placed? Were they faring better or worse than she?

"What are you thinking about?" Jakk asked. He hung back a little, as usual, but that didn't mean he didn't pay as close attention to her as Gav'n. His mismatched eyes made him fascinating and sexy. She wondered if women threw themselves at his feet.

"My shipmates. Will I be able to see them soon?"

Both Jakk and Gav'n's faces sobered. "No, *pashika*," Gav'n said. "The council decreed you shall not be able to see each other. They feel it is best for your adjustment and for the safety of our species."

Anger started slow but came on hot, simmering down in the pit of her belly. "What?"

"You heard him, Mira." Warning rang in Jakk's tone.

"That's not fair!" she spluttered. "They are my friends. I need to see them. They're like family to me—the only family I have!"

Jakk shook his head. "We're your family, now. We know it's painful, but you've been offered a chance to function in our society rather than be executed or remain in prison. But only if you follow the guidelines we provide you."

Hot tears of anger sprang to her eyes, and she turned away, back to the window.

Gav'n tugged her around, and she expected rebuke, but he folded her into his strong arms and held her against his massive chest, stroking the back of her head. "You'll adjust, little one."

Part of her wanted to push against him and fight and argue, but she didn't have the strength, and it felt so good to be held. She gave herself over to him, wetting his shirt with her tears. Almost immediately, warmth flanked her back, as well. Jakk stood behind her, closing the circle, or, rather, sandwiching her between the men. She felt small and helpless, like a child. But oddly protected.

We're your family, now.

She had to get used to the idea. She cried until her tears ran out. When she finished, Gav'n showed her to the bathroom and gave her a bag of toiletries they'd purchased for her. It included a laser-powered tooth-cleaning device, a hairbrush, and makeup in colors she would never in a million years wear. She smiled to herself, picturing the two men trying to pick out the cosmetics. Such big, capable men wouldn't have a clue what she liked. She wondered if they struggled that way with their nieces. Probably.

They'd said they needed her. Now that she was in their house and knew them a little better, she could see it was true. A trickle of warmth—the first tiny spark of hope she'd had since the crash—swirled in her chest.

Maybe she *would* find a place here. She'd never felt she belonged anywhere—not in her family of gorgeous super-geniuses, and not in college where she'd failed to make friends and build a social life like the rest of the students, choosing, instead, to stay locked away in labs working on the inventions she never brought to fruition. Getting the job with the colonization project had been the only bright spot in her murky career, but she and her shipmates hadn't made it. Now they were all stuck here as fosterlings to paternalistic aliens.

With fingers as big as human cocks.

3

W hen Mira emerged from the bathroom, Jakk picked up the tracking collar Gav'n had pilfered from the parole department at work. They'd had to resize it to fit her slender neck, but it allowed them to restrict her movements and track her at all times.

"Come here, little one. This is for you."

She balked, stopping in place, eyes flying wide. "What is it?"

"Your collar. We're going to have to leave you alone at times— possibly as soon as tomorrow, if Gav'n can't get out of his morning meeting, and we have an obligation to protect Endermere's citizens."

Her lip curled. "Protect Endermere's citizens?" Her hands flew to her slender hips, and one leg jutted out to the side in a clear notice of opposition. Damn, she was adorable. His balls were so blue they were purple from him studying every angle of her little naked body.

But he shouldn't have used those words because their little spit-fire was angry.

"So you still pretend we came here with the intent to *attack* Endermere?"

"Watch your tone with me," he warned. "Of course we don't believe that, but when you were given to our care, it was with the understanding we'd condition you to live in society. Leaving you alone to roam the streets on your first day out does not fit that agreement."

"So—what? I'm like a pet? Is there a leash, too?" Her eyes narrowed at the titanium collar that hinged in the front and locked in the back with a key. "Is that a tracking device? Or a shock collar?"

Of course she'd guess—their little engineer was as bright as they came. The citizens of Earth wouldn't send an idiot out on a colonization mission.

"Yes, both," he admitted.

"Fuck you," she hissed, hands clenching into fists as she backed up from him.

He stepped closer. "You've earned another consequence, Mira. This time it will be more than my hand."

Gav'n closed in on her from the other side with a deceptively casual approach.

"No." Her back hit the wall. Nowhere else to retreat.

Gav'n closed in, caging her between his two arms. "Punishment or collar first, Jakk?"

"Collar."

Gav'n pinned her wrists behind her head and pulled her away from the wall.

Jakk stepped in and clipped the collar in place, locking it at her nape and dropping the key in his pocket.

"Do you want to punish her?" Gav'n asked.

"Your choice." He and Gav'n rarely begrudged each other anything, operating almost from a single mind.

"I'll hold her again." His brother tugged her forward to the bed, where he sat and positioned her between his knees. "Bend over, like you did when Jakk removed your plug."

Mutiny lodged in the set of her jaw, the hardness of her fixed gaze on Gav'n's chest. His brother merely grinned. "Do you like to be forced, Mira?" Gav'n's easy tone made it sound like the punishment was a mere game, a form of play between the three of them. Which, in a way, it was. But with genuine consequences for all if they failed to win her submission.

He couldn't even think about her being taken from them. Already he'd grown attached—felt like she belonged to them. She was a gift in their lives. A once-in-a-lifetime chance for him to have everything he'd ever dreamed of. He sure as hell didn't want to screw things up.

Confusion flitted over Mira's face, and Gav'n grinned more broadly. "You do, don't you?" He gripped her nape and pulled her head down to his lap, forcing her to bend at the waist. "It's okay, *pashika*. I don't mind taking control, if that's easier for you. Until you're ready to yield. But consider this—you'll earn your little freedoms sooner if you submit.Fighting only makes us think we have reason to keep you locked up." He wrapped his fist in her hair and turned her face so he could see it. "Understand, little one?"

Jakk couldn't see her face, and he didn't hear an answer.

"She's ready," Gav'n said, releasing her hair.

He unbuckled his belt and slid it from the loops. It was an old belt—a favorite—of wide leather grown supple with wear. He wound the buckle end around his fist until only around eighteen inches remained. "Spread your legs, Mira."

She didn't move.

He snapped the leather across her pink bottom, and she shrieked, lurching forward into Gav'n's lap. "I asked you to spread your legs. I require your immediate obedience to all commands."

"Go fuck yourself," she growled, still dancing on her toes.

"No, no, baby." Gav'n's fingers threaded into her hair again. "You don't want to pick that fight with Jakk. Not in the position you're in. Open your legs and apologize for what you just said to him because it sounded like an insult to me."

She didn't move or speak. Jakk waited, sensing his brother was close to coaxing something from her, or he would've green-lighted Jakk to begin.

"I'm trying to save you a beating."

The scent of her tears reached his nose.

"Or do you need this beating?" Gav'n's soft-spoken words held only sympathy.

"I'm sorry, Jakk—Master," she choked out.

He kicked her feet apart. "You're forgiven. We know this is hard for you. Only twenty with my belt, and we're through."

He whipped her, going easy on the strokes. The balance of dominance with mercy would be crucial to win her surrender. He just hoped they hadn't gone too far either way.

She jerked and danced with each stroke but didn't cry out. He laid stripes up and down her ass and the backs of her legs, concentrating them in the place where her bottom curved into her thighs. When it was over, he dropped the belt and rubbed her ass, soothing the hot welts.

"Come here." This time he didn't want Gav'n to be the one to comfort her. He needed to do it himself. He pulled her up to stand, half expecting a fight. Her face was flushed, hair spilling over her eyes, jaw thrust forward at a sullen angle. "It's over," he murmured and pulled her into his arms.

She didn't return the embrace, but she didn't fight either. Her small body shook and trembled against his, spearing a new need to protect her that was foreign to him. The same need he'd felt in the prison, when threatening the guard. He had no doubt the guard had done exactly his duty, ensuring she ate enough food to maintain her health and well-being and punishing her when she refused, yet the idea of any other male touching her enraged him.

"Let's put you to bed, *pashika*. It's been a long evening. You'll feel better in the morning."

He released her, and she wobbled. She touched the collar around her neck with a grimace but turned and dutifully climbed up into the middle of the bed. Simply the sight of her lovely form, leggy and alluring, made his heart pick up speed. For the first time in his life, a female *belonged* in his bed.

A female who had just submitted to his discipline and received pleasure at his hands. He felt very lucky, even if she wasn't happy with them at the moment. He walked around to the bed and pulled the covers out from under her, waited until she climbed in, and rearranged them around her small body, tucking them in under her shoulders.

She curled up into a ball, her fists tucked up under her chin. He stroked a lock of hair from her face. "Gav'n and I still need to eat. Do you want me to wait until you've fallen asleep to leave?"

She'd been turned away from him, but now her sea-green eyes shot to his face. "Wha—? Um, no. Thanks."

He bent and kissed her forehead. "Thanks, *Master*," he corrected softly, not caring if she answered.

She closed her eyes and rolled away. "Thanks, Master." Only a whisper, but she'd spoken the words.

He squeezed her shoulder, too choked even to mutter, *Good girl.*

~.~

She woke nestled against a massive, warm body. Not just nestled—intertwined. Her head lay on a muscled shoulder, her palm on a chiseled chest. She'd tossed one of her legs over the male's hips and...*oh God*—yes, that was his very hard cock thickening against her bare sex. He wore some form of underwear. She still was naked.

She supposed she had to get used to nudity.

She opened her eyes. Which brother was it?

Jakk. For some reason, that surprised her. He hadn't struck her as the cuddly type, not that he'd lacked affection. Did he snuggle women after sex? The thought sent an entire tsunami of ideas and images screaming through her head. What it would be like to have sex—no, to *get fucked*—by Jakk? He'd be hard and demanding. Hold her down and thrust so deep she saw stars, leave her sore and aching.

Her core clenched, and her hips thrust toward him before she could stop herself.

Jakk stiffened as his cock surged against her leg. He lifted his head and looked at her. "You're awake, little one." He certainly sounded fully awake, as if he'd been lying there, waiting. "I didn't want to disturb you." He unceremoniously tipped her off his body and climbed swiftly out of bed, padding toward the bathroom. He wore only a pair of small, fitted boxer briefs, and his cock tented the front with an alarming length.

Damn, would that thing even fit inside her?

"I'm due at court today. Gav'n and I are juggling our time with you until you settle in." He stepped into the bathroom, and the sound of running water reached her.

He seemed to be in a rush. A curl of warmth threaded through her chest. Had he actually laid there afraid to wake her? Possibly making himself late?

When had anyone in her life been so thoughtful? Certainly her four perfect older sisters had never been quiet while she'd slept. Her roommates in college hadn't. Her boyfriends never cared. A little thing, but it touched her deeply.

Gav'n peeked in the door. He wore a crisp hunter-green uniform marked with crossed swords. It must be his police uniform. What did his job entail? She needed to learn as much as she could about her new situation, to figure out how to make life bearable. Finding and contacting her shipmates was at the top of her list.

"You're finally awake!" Gav'n said. "Come and have some break-fast. I have to talk to you about the way things are going to go today."

She slid out of bed, shivering at the loss of the warm covers and the lingering remains of Jakk's body heat.

"I'll turn the heat up. Gav'n, ever attentive, crooked a finger at her. "Better yet, I'll show you where the controls are so you can adjust it the way you want. Come here." She followed him into the hall, and he lifted a flap in the wall. Behind it glowed a basic digital control panel. The only problem was the markings were all in their language, which she couldn't read. The translator shot they'd given her allowed her to understand their language but didn't work on written words.

"This is the temperature." He pointed at the third control down. She memorized its location. He punched it several times. "This is

hotter." He held it down until a different word flashed. "This is cold-
er." She memorized the markings for hot and cold.

"Got it."

He grinned at her. "You're quick, little bird. Let's go downstairs.
We're going to introduce a new food this morning." He jogged down
the steps, and she followed.

On the table sat a bowl of the same beige grain they'd served her
in prison.

She stopped in her tracks. "Oh no." She shook her head. "No way.
I'm not eating that."

Gav'n watched her, face impassive. He was silent a moment.
When he drew a breath, she steeled herself for a threat. "Mira, would
you like to try that again? I take it you've had this cereal, and it didn't
agree with you?"

She nibbled her lip, already understanding what he wanted. "Yes,
Master."

"So, how should you speak to me when you tell me that?"

Her face burned. She hated being scolded like a child, almost as
much as she hated being wrong. "Respectfully. I'm sorry, Master."

"Try it again."

Pride warred with common sense. Part of her wanted to rebel,
simply because she felt humiliated at being corrected. The other part
knew she'd been peevish, and he didn't deserve it. She stared at a spot
beside the cereal. "Thank you for making me breakfast, Gav'n, but I
don't think that particular food works for my stomach."

"Better." He picked up the bowl of mush and dumped it down an
open hole in the sink. "Come here."

She walked into the kitchen with him. The door that appeared to
be a pantry or closet turned out to be the Pra'kirian version of a
refrigerator.

"What looks good to you?"

She scanned the food. Nothing, really. After daily bellyaches, she
was afraid to eat anything on Pra'kir.

"Do you want to stick with the *madlyne* fruit again? Did that go
down okay last night?"

Her tummy growled, but this time it was more from hunger than bad digestion. She nodded. "Yes, please. Master."

Gav'n's warm, rewarding smile did fluttery things to her chest. He handed her the fruit and pulled out a knife and cutting board.

Surprisingly, they trusted her with a knife. Not that she had any intention of trying to kill them both and escape into a busy city filled with aliens who considered her enemy number one. It might work well for picking the lock on her choker, though. She couldn't stand the thing. It was too tight, too heavy. Plus, the very idea of the thing pissed her off. If she was family, if they trusted her enough to care for the children of the household, they had to give her a little autonomy. Well, they didn't have to, but that's what she wanted. She'd never liked to be micromanaged.

Gav'n leaned a hip against the counter, folded his arms across his chest, and watched her work. Actually, she thought he might be watching her breasts, which tightened and grew heavy under his dark stare. It ought to bother her more than it did. Instead, she enjoyed the sense of power it gave her.

These males found her desirable. *Her*—the plain, less-than-brilliant sister who would never do important things like win the Nobel Prize in economics or represent their planet in United Galaxy discussions.

She lined the knife up over the fruit.

"Other way," Gav'n coached.

She turned it around and sliced through, squealing when a bit of bright-red juice hit her face.

Gav'n chuckled and leaned in, one large hand circling behind the small of her back. She spread her arms wide to keep from staining his uniform with the red juice. He pulled her into him and licked the spot of juice from her face. He smelled like cedarwood, or was it juniper? Something woodsy and masculine and wonderful. The warmth from his body radiated onto her bare skin.

Heat flooded her core. Another flick of his tongue—this time under her earlobe.

She drew in a breath and held it.

Slowly, he eased back and released her. "You taste delicious, little human."

Dizzy, she couldn't speak for a moment. When she regained her senses, she cleared her throat and pointed the tip of the knife at the swords on his shirt. "Is that the police symbol?"

"Military police, yes."

He seemed too laid-back to be a police commissioner. But, no, the rest of it fit. He was capable and quick-moving. Quite experienced at restraining bodies, as she'd discovered the night before.

Jakk appeared in his work clothes—a sleek suit and well-shined shoes—like the general magistrate had worn when he'd visited their cell to question them. "Gav'n's in charge of the entire force." A note of pride rang out in Jakk's voice.

"And Jakk holds one of the highest positions on Pra'kir, under the general magistrate and the Council of Nine."

"Impressive." She wondered if Jakk's important status was why he'd been given a human to foster. She finished chopping the fruit and washed her hands. "Are you both leaving?" She touched the collar around her neck.

"I have to go into court today, but Gav'n will be here with you, except for a short interval this morning when he will have to leave you alone." Jakk had turned stiff and formal again. It was hard to believe she'd just been snuggled up against this man.

"Okay." She sought a towel to dry her hands but didn't find one. Gav'n reached past her and hit a button under one of the cabinets, and a spray of warm air rushed out. "Ah. Thanks."

"Be good for Gav'n. I'll see you this afternoon."

She resisted the urge to walk over and kiss him goodbye. The domestic scene seemed to call for something of the sort, but she didn't know the proper protocol. Besides, she wasn't sure they deserved her affection. Not when they had her naked and wearing a pet collar. Not after all the punishments she'd endured for not acting slave-like.

Jakk did seem to be hesitating, though, as if waiting for something, or was reluctant to leave. He turned and walked stiffly toward the front door.

"Have a good day," she sang out, remembering what her parents used to say when one of them left the house.

He stopped and turned back, a small smile curving his lips and transforming his wooden expression. It sent a spike of warmth shooting through her. "You too, *pashika*."

She smiled back before ducking her head. Damn, she shouldn't cave so easily to the charm of these two brothers. Where was her pride? Self-respect?

She'd clearly lost her mind—and herself—under one night of Jakk and Gav'n's erotic handling. They'd lulled her into the belief living here in Pra'kir might work for her. But, deep down, she knew it wasn't true. It was still a prison, just a much nicer one.

~.~

IT TOOK all Gav'n's self-control not to follow Mira into the shower and wash her beautiful body himself. But, if he did, she'd end up with her little hands pressed against the marble wall and his cock pounding her from behind until she screamed herself hoarse. And that would be against the rules.

Although Jakk was more worried about rules than he was. He knew their little human wanted them. He'd smelled her arousal, watched her sneak glances at their bodies. He'd seen the way her nipples puckered every time she got close to one of them. Hell, she'd already begged prettily for her climaxes yesterday. Getting her to beg for their cocks shouldn't be too hard a feat.

But Jakk was right. The request had to come from her. If their treatment of her ever came into question, they needed to have a clear conscience on that point.

So, instead of barging into her shower time, he lounged on top of the bedcovers, ankles crossed, hands behind his head, waiting for her to return, dewy and clean.

He wasn't disappointed. She emerged with a towel wrapped around her midsection, eyelashes clinging together. What about seeing a female wet made her even sexier? Her long hair fell over her shoulders, eyes bright against her rosy cheeks.

He pulled a frown. "Drop the towel, little one. You know we want you naked during your conditioning."

She rolled her eyes, but he caught the movement of her swallow and the flutter of her increased pulse as she tugged off the towel.

"Better."

Actually, it was divine. Her small body was like a work of art, every line graceful. One breast was slightly larger than the other, an asymmetry that only made her more perfect. He'd noticed that morning she still bore a few marks on her ass from her whipping the night before, and he had to admit he liked seeing evidence of their dominance, liked knowing she was theirs to correct.

Of course, what he liked best was their no clothing rule. Having Mira bared to them at all times had been a stroke of pure genius—other than the resulting permanent hard-ons he and his brother sported.

"We did, actually, order you some clothing." He remained lounging on the bed, willing his straining cock to relax. "Not much because we weren't sure whether it would fit." He pointed to a storage tub stacked with a few items of clothing on the floor of the closet. "Take a look. It's from an adolescent line, but we tried not to get anything too childish."

She held up a navy-blue jumper and made a face. "This isn't childish?"

He chuckled. "I'll bet it will be cute on you—try it on."

Her eyes narrowed. "Next, you'll want a strip tease."

He didn't understand the translation for *strip tease*, but he grinned anyway. "Don't get sassy. I like to punish naughty humans as much as Jakk does."

She muttered something that sounded like, "Smug person-conceived-out-of-wedlock," but picked up the jumper and pulled it on over her head. It only came to mid-thigh, framing her long, slender legs and giving her a sexy yet innocent appearance. She tugged at the hem, as if the dress might magically grow if she willed it to. "It's too small."

Way too small. Her breasts stretched the fabric in front, which hugged her narrow waist and flared again at the hips. His cock strained against his pants. "It's perfect."

She picked up a pair of panties.

"No panties. No bras." He patted his knee.

She shook her head.

"One...two..."

She flounced over and threw herself onto his lap, lips set in a mulish line.

He tapped them, circling her waist with his arm. "Mira, one more sign of attitude from you and you'll get the belt. I'm losing patience."

She averted her gaze.

"I have a meeting this morning. It shouldn't take too long. You may wear clothing while I'm gone—minus the panties—but you may not leave the townhouse. The clothing will come off when I return. Understand?"

She waited a beat before muttering, "Yes, Master."

"The collar will prevent you from leaving the house unless we disable the shock function. There is a safety mechanism in case of fire. The alarm will shut off the shocker. It will also track you. When the girls come, you will be responsible for taking them to and from school. If you go anywhere except the places we've agreed, you will be punished. *Severely.*"

Her eyes darted to his then away. The first thread of concern found its way into his chest. His detective instincts told him she'd already been considering her escape.

He gripped her chin and turned her face to his. "Mira, the people of Endermere believe you are dangerous. Jakk and I know that's not true, but if anyone saw you alone, there's a chance they might attack in self-defense. It's not safe for you to be out unaccompanied. Not to mention, Jakk and I would be in trouble with the Council of Nine for not keeping you under lock and key. Monitoring your movements is as much for your safety as it is part of our responsibility as your foster family."

She nibbled her lip, a crease growing between her brows.

He rubbed it with the pad of his thumb. "Don't worry. Eventually, things will settle down. They'll stop showing that damn clip of your crash landing, and the neighbors will get used to seeing you around and learn you're harmless. Until then, it's necessary to restrict your movements."

She sighed.

"You're a smart woman. You know we're right in this."

"I understand your logic, yes. That doesn't mean I like it." She darted a quick glance at him. "Master."

His lips quirked into a smile, he squeezed her hip. "I love hearing you call me that."

Surprise flitted over her face. He stroked her cheek and leaned forward to claim her mouth.

She stiffened at first, but he swept his tongue along the seam of her lips, coaxing her to life. After a moment, her lips moved back with a tentative sweetness that turned his insides molten.

"Beautiful girl," he murmured when they broke apart. He stroked her face again. "I'm so glad you've come to live with us. We'll work hard to make you happy here, I promise."

Confusion clouded her face—hope warring with doubt, if he had to name what he saw there.

"Give us a chance. Yield to our will. Submit to our guidance, and we'll give you everything we have."

She surged to her feet, and he let her go. Stumbling, she found her way to the window and stood facing it.

After a moment, he came to stand behind her, touching her shoulders.

He felt her questions, her confusion, but doubted any words would answer them. Nothing he could say would soften the ache of homesickness or her loss of control over her life.

She faced a lifetime as their prisoner. He and Jakk had the impossible task of ensuring she understood her restricted place in their society, and also ease the pain of it. Would their sexual attentions be enough to distract her?

Somehow, with all he saw going on behind those beautiful eyes, he doubted it.

4

Mira stood in front of the mirror in the bathroom, craning her neck forward as she reached her arms behind her like a contortionist. She'd managed to get the lock pin to move, just a little. The damn collar was so fitted, she couldn't even swivel it around to put the lock in the front and make it easier to pick.

Yes, she understood why Jakk and Gav'n believed she needed to wear it. And she disagreed. So, while Gav'n was at his meeting, she was damn well going to take it off. She needed to practice removing it, so if—no, *when*—she managed to locate her fellow shipmates, she'd be able to slip away and visit them without being traced. Not to mention any other time she needed a bit of freedom. Being held prisoner—even if the two men who thought they owned her knew how to play her body like a fine-tuned instrument—didn't work for her.

A little more...almost...damn.

She shook her arms out and rolled her neck. If it took the entire time Gav'n was gone, she would figure out how to open this flipping lock.

She threaded the narrow knife blade into the lock once more, seeking the inner pin with the tip. *There.* She nudged it to the right...*a little more...just a bit and...success!* The collar fell open, and she caught it, bringing it in front of her eyes to investigate. Even as a child, she'd always loved to take things apart and see how they worked. Her sisters had made fun of her tinkering and, when she'd declared her aspirations to become an engineer instead of something more glamorous or prestigious, had rolled their eyes and said it figured.

Perhaps she could take the collar apart to deactivate the shock function and remove the tracker. She'd leave the tracking software on, but store it someplace at home when she left to go places. She tucked it into the rather too-small pocket of the jumper and went in search of tools.

For the first time since their crash, she had a moment of autonomy. It felt delicious to have the freedom to investigate the townhouse on her own. She tripped down the stairs and started in the kitchen, opening drawers and cabinets, examining all the foreign products. From there, she tried what appeared to be an office in the room beside the girls'.

Nothing.

Where would tools be? Had there been a "garage" or workshop type area on the street level where they parked the shuttles? Would anyone see her if she slipped outside to look?

No better way to find out than to try. She pulled the choker out of her pocket and dropped it onto the little bench underneath a row of hooks jammed with children's jackets and school bags beside the front door. She put her ear to the door to listen.

No sound of anyone.

She slid the lock open and cracked the door, peeking out.

All clear.

Slipping out, she ran on bare feet down the back stairwell until she reached the ground floor.

Voila! It turned out there was a shed she hadn't noticed when they arrived, tucked in the corner of the itty bitty parking spot cum yard.

She tried the door, but it was locked. Hopefully, it was as primitive as the lock on her collar, and she could simply pick it. She went back up the stairs for the knife, her bare feet silent on the wooden steps. As she reached the door, the sound of a shuttle pulling into the yard below reached her ears.

Gav'n! She slipped inside, raced upstairs to their bedroom, and threw herself on the bed, as if she'd been lounging there.

The door opened downstairs.

Fuck. Her hand flew to her neck. She'd left the collar on the table below.

"Mira?" Judging from the sound of Gav'n's outraged roar, he'd seen it. "Mira!" he shouted again before she even had a chance to think about answering.

Heart pounding, she climbed off the bed. "I'm—"

"Mira!" A pitch of desperation tinged his roar now. His footsteps pounded up the stairs, shaking the old walls with their thunder.

"I'm right he—"

He arrived in the doorway, the collar clutched in his hand, eyes wild. They widened when he saw her, and then he sagged against the doorframe. The relief only lasted a moment, though, replaced by fury. "What in the *hell* is going on?" He shook the fist with the collar, advancing slowly toward her.

Lying seemed fruitless. What could she possibly say? It fell off?

She opted for stubborn, instead. Folding her arms over her chest, she lifted her chin. "I told you I don't like it. It's too heavy, too tight, and I don't like being a prisoner in my own home."

Her own home. Did she really consider this place to be her home already?

Interest also flickered on Gav'n's expression before it hardened into something more resolute.

He took another step toward her, face dark and dangerous. She saw the cop in him now—he appeared lethal. It didn't hurt that he was a foot-and-a-half taller than her. "So what? You picked the lock?"

She nodded.

He put his hands on his hips and gazed upward, as if imploring some higher power for patience. Did Pra'kirians believe in a higher power? She made a mental note to ask later on.

"And you left it there for me to see? You wanted me to know our device can't hold you?"

She hoped he didn't notice the flush creeping up her neck. This part of the story, she definitely wanted to keep a secret. She swallowed and nodded.

His mouth firmed. "Clothes off." The hardness of his tone snapped like a whip.

Punishment.

What would it be this time? The belt? Or something worse?

She considered refusing the order, but even if she was willing to run away—which she wasn't, not without a plan— she'd never outrun Gav'n in a race. Her only choice was to strip and accept his discipline. She pulled off the jumper.

Gav'n tossed several pillows in the middle of the bed. "Lie over them." He sounded grim.

She obeyed, placing her hips over the stack of padding so it lifted her ass in the air.

Gav'n stalked to the closet and emerged carrying several strips of silky fabric—some kind of formal men's tie, perhaps? He used one to bind her ankles together and the second to tie her wrists behind her back.

"Since you won't wear your collar, I'll have to keep you tied up. Remember this was your choice when your arms fall asleep, little girl."

She bit back the *fuck you* rising to her lips.

Gav'n went to the closet again, and this time returned with a thin cane.

Oh shit. Her bottom clenched reflexively.

He rested one knee on the bed and clasped one of her bound hands in his larger one. The move surprised her, but before she had a chance to lift her head and look at him, the cane swished through the air and landed across her buttocks like a line of pure fire.

She screamed, bowing up in shock.

"That's for defiance." He struck again.

She panted with a moan of pain.

"And that's for being too damn clever for your own good." Another line of fire.

She gasped, tears smarting her eyes.

He whipped her again. "*That's* for scaring the crap out of me, thinking you'd run away." Another wicked line of fire.

She screamed, certain she couldn't take any more. It was so much worse than the belt.

But the cane swished through the air again and landed mercilessly. "And that's for being sweet enough to stay." His voice grew soft on the last words, and he leaned over and kissed her heaving back. Was that gratitude or affection in his voice?

The cane clattered to the hardwood floor and sounded like it rolled under the bed. If she were smart, she'd retrieve it and burn it before he remembered where it had gone. Her entire ass was on fire, her body shaking.

Something beeped, and Gav'n muttered a curse her translator didn't get—something like *volchek*. "What is it?" he snapped, and she realized he was speaking into his communicator.

"Commissioner, I'm sorry to bother you, but we have a suspected bomb threat at Endermere Academy for Higher Learning. The team is responding, but I thought you'd want to know."

Gav'n cursed again. "I'll meet them there." He disconnected. "*Volchek. Volchek. Volchek.* Now, what in the hell am I going to do with you? Hmm?" He slapped her throbbing ass. "Obviously, you can't be left alone for even a minute."

She heard him rummage in the closet again, and when he returned, he had another silk tie. He unfastened her ankles from each other and quickly tied one to each bed post, so she lay with her hips still lifted and her legs spread wide, pussy exposed.

"I would have preferred to stay and watch this particular part of your punishment, but I am needed elsewhere." He moved with quick efficiency.

"What part...*ooh!*" She tried to tighten her ass when a glop of something cool dropped between her cheeks.

Gav'n rubbed it in a tight circle around her anus and then pressed a plug against her opening.

She attempted to kick her legs, but with her ankles tied wide, they didn't budge. "What are you doing?" she spluttered.

"Making you a sorry little girl. I don't have time to go slow, so open for me now." He pressed the object with more insistence and, against her will, the tight ring of muscles yawned to admit the plug. No—it wasn't a plug. It was worse—a vibrator! The phallus hummed to life, stimulating every nerve ending in her pelvic floor and inside her ass.

"Ohhhh," she moaned.

"I'm not finished." His fingers probed her pussy. "Good, you're already wet." He thrust a second, larger vibrator inside her channel and set it to hum, as well. "Don't even think about moving from this position." He slapped her poor, throbbing ass and she heard him leave the room.

"Jakk, I have a situation," his terse voice sounded from the stairs as he left her there, in total wanton misery.

~.~

JAKK'S HEAD swam and he had to lean against the bedroom door frame to keep from lurching. Their little human lay naked on her belly, legs tied wide, striped ass raised up on pillows, vibrating dildos buzzing in both her anus and dripping pussy.

She hadn't heard him come in, and the blankets were clenched in her teeth as she moaned a repetitive, plaintive cry. The scent of her arousal filled the room, and energy snapped and crackled, rebounding off the walls and sending waves of heat cascading through his body. His cock was harder than a rock.

"I heard you were a very naughty girl."

Her head snapped up, and she twisted, trying to see over her shoulder. Her eyes were glassy and dilated, cheeks flushed bright-red.

"Jakk, Jakk, Jakk," she breathed in a chant. "Oh God, please...*please.*"

He was afraid to move from the doorway. If he got even a foot closer to her, he'd lose all control and take her without any consent.

"Were you naughty, Mira?"

"Yes. I'm sorry." She shifted her upper body, as much as she was able to with her hands tied behind her back. "I hate the collar. I took it off. But I didn't run away. I'm still here. Please, doesn't that count for something?"

The desperate plea in her voice finally got through his fog of lust, and he walked to the bed, untying first one ankle then the other.

She humped the pillows, her welted ass squirming and wriggling.

He inhaled slowly through his nose, trying to clear his head. The scent of her arousal only made it worse, though. He pulled the vibrator out of her pussy and switched it off. It was coated with her sweet juices.

"Jakk," she moaned.

He removed the anal vibrator and switched it off then untied her wrists.

She whined and moved them slowly up by her head. A wild, animal-like expression painted her face. Her little body shook, and she breathed in short pants.

"You look like one very sorry little girl." He ran his thumb down her cheek.

She mumbled something including Gav'n's name, but he didn't catch the rest. He roughly rubbed her ass, punishing and soothing at the same time. She moaned, lifting her curves into his hand.

His communicator beeped with a call from Gav'n. He fit an earpiece into his ear so Mira wouldn't hear Gav'n. "I'm home."

"Is she all right?"

"She didn't go anywhere, if that's what you mean. I don't know if she's all right. She's feverish and shaky."

"She needs you to fuck her."

His cock surged at his brother's words, but he steeled himself against the urge to do exactly that.

"Ask her. Say, Do you need your master's cock?"

Only his own desperate need prompted him to follow his brother's urging. "Mira," he said hoarsely. "Do you need your master's cock?"

"Yes. Yes, sir. Yes, Master." She spread her legs the way they'd been when he walked in.

He disconnected the call with Gav'n and tossed the communicator onto the couch. In a nanosecond, he had his pants down and his aching cock free. He climbed over Mira and rubbed the head of his cock over her slick entrance.

"Bad girl," he said thickly, his tongue tangling as his cock inched into her hot, wet channel. Her muscles squeezed him. "Oh, Mira," he groaned. "I knew you'd be tight, but I had no idea it would be this good."

He tried to hold back because she was so much smaller and it was their first time, but she arched her ass even higher than the pillows, wantonly begging for it. He gripped her hips, unable to restrain himself. He manipulated her body with his hands, alternately lifting and lowering her pelvis over his cock then bracing her pelvis for him to pound into her, his flesh slapping her heated ass.

The noises she made destroyed him. Little grunts. Mewls. Choked cries. His fingers dug into her flesh, cock thrust and retreated like his life depended on it. He knew he was too rough with her, but he couldn't contain his lust, his desire. She'd been a torture to him since the moment they'd stripped her naked the night before. He'd spent the night feverish with desire from having her lush little body nestled up against his.

His vision closed into a narrow tunnel. Nothing but pure desire and the need to quench it drove him. His thighs flexed, balls tightened. Stars sparked in the periphery. "Mira, yes, yes, hell yes!" he roared, driving so deep inside, he flattened her to her belly, and still he wanted deeper, deeper...to the depths of her soul to mark her forever with his seed. Cum shot down his shaft, hot streams filling her.

Ecstatic silence closed in on him, shut down his senses. After ages, or maybe only a few moments, he became aware of his little human panting beneath him, their bodies so tight he didn't know where his ended and hers began.

Aaaand he was probably suffocating her. He sure as hell hoped he hadn't hurt her. Shit—what if he had? He lifted away from her, easing out of her glorious channel with a groan.

"Mira," he rasped, settling beside her. Her blonde hair swooped and twisted on the bedcovers, fanning out from her face, still hidden deep in blanket.

She made a faint "hmmm" sound.

"Sweet little human." He stroked his large hand down her slender back. "I was too rough with you. I'm sorry. I couldn't control myself. I've needed to do that since the moment you came here."

He might have worried at her refusal to lift her head, but she made a little swishing motion with her ass, a little wiggle he took to be contentment. He'd feel better if she'd show him her face, promise him she was unhurt and didn't hold a grudge for the way he'd lost control, but he settled for stroking and petting her.

After a few minutes, her breath slowed, and he realized she must have dropped into sleep. His heart twisted. How could it be he'd already come to care about her so much it hurt?

He loved her. Would she ever love him? Even if she got over the fact he was little more than her glorified prison guard, there was his deformity. No Prak'irian female could love a man like him. The best he could hope for was Mira to tolerate his presence and accept what he had to offer.

No, he'd better put out the little spark of hope lodged in his chest, threatening to catch flame and grow ever brighter.

She still hadn't met the girls. And her rebellion had not been quelled nearly enough for him to feel comfortable she wouldn't bolt at the first opportunity.

They had huge hurdles ahead of them just to coexist together. He'd better forget about love.

~.~

MIRA WOKE TO A DARKENED ROOM, her stomach rumbling angrily. She hadn't slept so deeply since their cryosleep on the ship.

She pushed up to sit. *Ow.* Her weight on her tender ass brought back Gav'n's caning and Jakk's rough fucking. It had been...well, she didn't even know how to assign meaning to it.

The door pushed open and Gav'n came in, handsome in his still-crisp uniform, and carrying a tray of food. "*Pashika*, you're awake."

She licked her lips, despite her reservations about how the food would go down. "Yes, Master."

He sat on the edge of the bed and slid the tray in front of her, balancing it on her thighs. "Hungry, love? You missed lunch. Jakk prepared you a variety of things to try—all foods known to be gentle on the stomach."

She examined the tray, which held a bowl of steaming soup, a small plate of a sliced green vegetable, and the *madlyne* fruit. "Thank you both," she murmured, and picked up a spoon to sample the soup.

Gav'n's eyes were soft as he watched her. He reached out and attempted to detangle her hair with his fingers, but caught a knot and pulled. "Sorry."

She smiled, and their gazes caught, held. Sudden shyness crept over her—odd after what Gav'n had already seen and done with her. She dropped her eyes to the food.

The soup was salty and flavorful. "Mmm," she murmured as the juices from her stomach surged with enthusiasm. Suddenly starving, she picked up the bowl and drank from the side, draining the entire thing.

Catching Gav'n's shocked expression, she grinned and wiped a drip from the corner of her mouth. "It's not polite on Earth, either."

He threw back his head and laughed, the deep rich sound warming her.

She handed the tray back to him. "I don't think I should try anything else until I see how this goes down."

"Very well." He took the tray and set it on the bedside table. His eyes glittered as he considered her.

"You were a good girl to take your master's cock like you did this afternoon."

Take your master's cock.

The words alone had her pussy clenching and her belly fluttering.

"Jakk said he was too rough with you. I need to inspect." He reached for her, pulling her onto his lap.

She struggled, but he easily mastered her, flipping her over his lap and slapping her raw ass.

"Your masters are responsible for your well-being. That means this little body is under our charge. We must know what's going on with it at all times."

He ran his hand lightly over her welts, circling her bottom with a soothing caress. "You have a perfect little ass, Mira. And, I have to confess, I love to see my marks on it. I like knowing you're subject to my rules and discipline."

Her belly twisted with that pronouncement, but the protest inside her didn't find its way out. Possibly because it wouldn't be entirely honest.

He pried her thighs apart and traced one fingertip along the seam of her pussy. "A little swollen from use. Is it terribly sore?"

"A little. Not terribly." The memory of the normally reserved Jakk pounding into her, his lust unchecked, sent fresh arousal snaking through her core. The sense of power in knowing she evoked that much passion from him more than made up for his roughness.

He traced up from her slit to the crack of her ass, wiggling the pad of his digit over her anus. "When you take my cock, it will be here, Mira."

She squeezed her cheeks, clamping them closed on his finger.

He laughed and slapped the back of her thigh. "You will like it, I promise."

Fuck that! Er...no—never fuck that.

He rolled her over and gathered her into his arms. Amusement sparkled in his eyes. "You will beg me for it, *pashika*."

"No, I won't." She let her stubborn show.

He touched the tip of her nose. "With respect."

"Master."

He palmed one of her breasts. "You will," he murmured. Once more she was reminded of the steel beneath Gav'n's seemingly laid-back demeanor. "We still have a problem, little human."

She grimaced.

"Jakk and I thought we could leave you home alone with the collar on. Now that we know you can remove it, we can't. Are we going to have to tie you up every time we leave?"

She shook her head, the edge of panic creeping in. The hour she'd spent tied up alone with the vibrators in her had nearly killed her. "I won't remove it, Master."

Gav'n looked regretful. "I wish I believed you, *pashika*, but I can't. We'll have to find some other way to track you, perhaps a surgical implant."

"No! I'll leave it on. I promise." She chewed her lip, wishing she hadn't colossally screwed herself by getting caught that afternoon. She needed her freedom. She needed to see her shipmates—if for nothing else, so she didn't feel so damn alone and strange anymore.

~.~

JAKK SAT behind the wheel of his sister's shuttle and gave Mira the rundown on how everything worked. She'd slept between them again, leaving him as needy for her as he'd been the previous morning, despite the fact he'd taken her hard the night before.

His poor brother still sported a set of the bluest balls on the planet.

At least Mira had clothing on at the moment—minus underclothes.

"You set the destination here. The girls' academy is already programmed in, see?" He scrolled through the destinations, which he'd limited to the grocery store, home, and the school. Even the grocery store pushed the limits. If anyone saw Mira out unattended, they would absolutely panic. Most of the general public believed she and her cohorts were dangerous aliens intent on waging war with their planet.

Which still left them with the dilemma of controlling her movements. Neither he nor Gav'n believed her claim she wouldn't remove the collar again. If she knew how to do it once, she'd do it again. He didn't believe a simple caning would stop that, no matter what she promised. But he and Gav'n simply couldn't be with her every hour of the day. It defeated the purpose of having her as a support to their family.

Mira tapped her fingers on the dash, showing her impatience.

He flicked through the news feed stations, seeking out the only one that played music, instead of news. "Do you like music?"

She winced. "This is music?"

"Is it not beautiful to you?"

"Is it beautiful to you?" She sought his eyes in the rearview mirror.

"I love it," he admitted. Music had always been the thing that soothed, a friend when everyone besides his twin shunned him.

"Are there other music stations?"

He shook his head. Music had always been the least popular art form on Pra'kir, and it had gone even further out of fashion in the past twenty years. He switched off the station. "We don't have to listen. I know most don't love it the way I do." He shoved his seat backward. "Come here."

She shrieked when he lifted her by the armpits and settled her on his lap to drive. Gav'n had made the rule she couldn't wear panties, so her ass was bare under the too-short jumper. It felt divine against his perma-hard cock, and her exotic scent filled his nostrils.

"Why am I on your lap?" she protested. "I can drive this thing myself. I don't need you to hold the wheel."

He wrapped a fist in her hair and tugged her head back until it rested against his shoulder. "Mira, do not get sassy with me."

To his surprise, the scent of her arousal filled the cabin of the vehicle. Did pulling her hair turn her on?

"Ow." She squirmed, making his cock even more eager to strip the layer of fabric lying between them and impale that tight little pussy.

He waited.

"I'm sorry, Master."

He instantly rewarded her good behavior by releasing her hair. "You will drive and I will oversee the driving. Once you have gained my trust, I will allow you to drive on your own. Understand?"

"Yes, Master." There was sullenness to her tone, but he let it go.

"Start the shuttle."

She didn't require additional instructions on starting the shuttle, nor on maneuvering it out of the tiny parking space and into the alley. He lifted a finger to direct her toward the speedrails, but she'd already found the tracks, using the proper signaling.

Good girl.

She gave the shuttle too much power getting on the tracks and jumped them the first time, but before he reached to steady the wheel, she'd corrected the course and the shuttle settled, the auto-route initiating.

She shifted her ass over his cock, and this time he was certain it was on purpose.

"Human, if you don't want me to shove you up over the wheel and unbutton my pants so you can ride my cock all the way to the school, you'd better stop that squirming."

He swore her pussy transmitted dampness onto his pants. He reached around and pinched one of her nipples.

"I've never had a female so at my disposal before." He immediately kicked himself for saying so. She wasn't technically at their disposal. They were supposed to be operating with her consent.

But it seemed she wasn't offended. "Why not?"

He stiffened. "Isn't it obvious?"

She twisted to face him then stopped when he growled at the way her ass moved and she sought his eyes in the rearview mirror instead. "No."

He couldn't help the way his entire insides solidified and turned cold. It was the defense mechanism he'd employed since he was old enough to understand what made him different. Gav'n said it made him too stiff, too wooden, but it was out of his control.

"I really don't know. I'm not a Pra'kirian. Where are your females? Do you not marry?"

"Pra'kirians mate, yes. But I will not."

Her blank curiosity didn't appear faked. "Why? Judges can't marry? Can Gav'n?"

The pain he'd long ago resolved himself to surfaced, and he allowed it to wash over him. "Gav'n will most likely marry and have his own family."

"So you still haven't explained. Why won't you?"

His jaw locked. He had to work to pry it open. "My eyes."

Now she did swivel on his lap, shifting until she almost faced him. "I still don't understand. It's a genetic thing? Does your eye color come with sterility?"

He gave a bitter laugh. "No, Mira. But no female in her right mind would ever choose to bond herself to me. I'm a misfit."

Mira's mouth dropped open. Her face went pale and then flushed with color. "That's the stupidest thing I've ever heard," she spluttered.

The shuttle whipped off the main tracks onto the side road in front of the girls' academy and slowed to a stop in the drop off lane. "Destination reached," an automated female voice told them.

He didn't like Mira's looking at him like that. Was it with pity?

A fierce expression crossed her face. "Do you know what we do on Earth with a male with eyes like you?"

Dread flushed through him. Did she despise his appearance, too? He steeled himself for her pronouncement.

She unzipped the front of her jumper, allowing her breasts to spring free. Shocked, he took a quick look out the windows, but no one was around—he'd timed their trip during the lightest traffic during the middle of the school day.

She climbed into the passenger seat on her knees then bent over and unfastened his pants.

He groaned as his cock sprang free. Horrified at being in front of the academy with his cock out, he hit the button for home.

Crouched with her ass in the air toward the passenger window, Mira gripped his cock at the base and lowered her head. He groaned the moment the head of his cock met her soft lips then bathed in the moist heat of her mouth.

"Mira...*oh*."

She took him deep into her throat then plastered her tongue against his length as she sucked hard, drawing the blood down his shaft. At this rate, he wouldn't last five seconds.

"Mira. Holy hell, woman. You're killing me."

She lifted her eyes, lips stretching into a smile around his cock. "Mmm," she hummed as she lowered her mouth over his cock again.

He closed his eyes, unable to take in the scenery whizzing by at the same time a beautiful blonde alien made love to his cock.

She picked up speed, bobbing her head while she dragged her fist up and down his cock, making it feel like she'd taken the whole length of it into her little mouth.

"Oh...*oh*. Yes." How did he get so lucky? Was this truly happening to him? It sure as hell was the first time in his life he'd ever had more action from a female than his brother had. And he didn't feel the least bit guilty, either.

He buried his fingers in her hair, urging her over his cock faster, deeper. "Mira, yes! Oh hell yes. Yes!"

He slammed his feet against the floorboard and jacked his hips up, choking Mira as his cock shoved deep into her throat. Hot streams of his seed shot into her mouth, but his beautiful human didn't pull off. She kept sucking and swallowed his offering, licking him clean.

He closed his eyes, soaking up the moment, wanting to remember it for the rest of his life. He didn't even care to analyze what Mira had meant by it. All he knew was she was the best thing that had ever happened to him, and he needed to show her that in a variety of ways that all ended with her screaming a climax until her voice went hoarse.

Mira sat up. He pried his eyes open to see her smug smile, right when the shuttle exited the speedway and sent them hurtling down the side street toward the townhouse. He took over the controls to maneuver them into the alley and park the vehicle.

"Naughty girl," he rumbled as he opened her door and offered a hand to help her out, careful to zip her jumper before their nosy old neighbor, Linat, saw. When she stood, he tossed her over his shoulder and carried her, kicking, up the stairs. "Now I'm going to have to spend all afternoon making sure you know how much I—we—appreciate you."

In their room, he flicked on the small device that broadcast music, turning it up as loud as it went.

"Don't you have speakers for that thing?" Mira muttered.

He didn't understand the word *speaker*.

"The sound quality is awful. Does it go any louder?"

"This is as loud as it goes," he said.

He plopped her in the center of the bed. Three hours before he had to leave to drive out to his parents and pick up the girls, and he had one aroused human female to satisfy.

5

Mira paced the living room, examining every object on every shelf.

"Relax. They're only children." Gav'n came up behind her and touched her shoulders. After a wild afternoon of lovemaking, Jakk had left to pick up their nieces and bring them home. She was more nervous about meeting the children than she had been about her "conditioning" by Jakk and Gav'n.

That had turned out to be bearable. And somewhat enjoyable, if she was completely honest. Not that she thought they should have the right to physically discipline her, but the line between punishment and pleasure had blurred right from the beginning, making it hard for her to hate one without rejecting the other.

Gav'n's warm hands stroked down her sides then up the back of her short dress to palm her ass. "How's your ass today? I heard you were a good girl all day. No punishments. Did you take your master's cock again?"

Her pulse quickened. Heat pooled between her legs. "Yes," she whispered.

He insinuated a finger between her cheeks and rubbed a tiny circle over her anus. "Are you ready to take me here?"

"No, Master," she choked out.

He pushed her torso down until her hands connected with the back of the sofa, then he slid the hem of her dress up to her back. Her ass was bare underneath it, as he required, although he had allowed her to don a slightly longer skirt before the girls arrived.

The girls. Oh shit. What if they walked in on this? Surely Gav'n wouldn't let that happen....would he?

He peppered her ass with swift spanks, making her yelp because her bottom was still sore from the caning the day before.

"What's that for?"

"To remind you who's in charge. Spread your legs." His voice sounded thick.

She widened her stance. His fingers quested between her legs, dipping into her swollen, dripping pussy. Jakk had spent hours keeping her on the edge of an orgasm before he'd fucked her and let her climax, but she still seemed to crave more.

"I guess I'll have to take your pussy tonight."

He said it like a statement, but she had the sense he was waiting for her agreement. She arched her back in invitation. He stroked two hands down her outer thighs. "Good girl." She heard the rustle of his clothing, and then his cock prodded her entrance.

Not once had Jakk worn a condom. She didn't know if they even existed on this planet. She ought to have the birth control conversation with them, except she was half afraid of what they would tell her. Was she obligated to be their breeder?

And she didn't want to admit it because it was flat-out nuts, but some tiny part of her loved the idea of having their baby. Making their family a real family.

Not that the girls weren't real.

The girls!

But she forgot her anxiety over the girls as Gav'n wedged his huge cock inside her. Although she was sore from so much sexual activity, the pleasure by far outweighed any discomfort.

"Oh, *pashika*. You are as tight and perfect as Jakk promised." He gripped her hips and eased in and out. "I could do this all day."

"No...you really couldn't. The girls are on their—"

He covered her mouth with one hand, bumping his loins against her ass with short thrusts. "Hush. You'll take my cock whenever and wherever I say, little one." The hand slid from her mouth to her throat, closing lightly around her neck.

Her pussy clenched around his length, even as her mind rebelled at his words. She tried to rally her thoughts, but his cock had found her G-spot, and pleasure spun and spiraled through her like a top out of control. "On Earth, we don't allow children to see—"

His hand clapped over her mouth again. "We don't here, either. So you'd better satisfy your master quickly, because if they see us like this, I'll have to punish you long and hard."

Oh God. Why did his mean talk make her knees go weak?

He picked up one of her knees, changing the angle so he could pummel deeper into her.

She gasped, her other knee buckling, her vision going fuzzy. "Gav'n," she choked.

"Take it," he growled, thrusting harder and harder until she thought he would knock the breath out of her.

She came close to climaxing, but he pulled out and spanked her, fast and hard.

"Ack! What's that for? Why—"

"Hush, human. I already told you, I don't need a why. Having a hot red ass helps you remember who your masters are."

The *fuck you* that sprang to mind was only halfhearted because, in fact, the spanking felt delicious. Yes, it hurt. It totally hurt—but his mastery over her left her panting for more.

He stopped and spun her around to face him, settling her over his cock. With his palms under her ass, he lifted and lowered her, bounced her into the air, sending her up and down over his huge cock, driving deeper into her channel with each bounce.

"Yes, *yes*, little human!" he roared, moving her at a frenetic pace now.

"Yes," she agreed, eyes rolling back in her head.

Gav'n gave an animalistic bellow and buried deep, filling her with his hot seed.

Her pussy clenched, her own climax arriving moments later, wiping all anxiety from her mind and body. At that moment, she knew nothing but Gav'n. Her breath mingled with his; her arms twined around his neck.

He nibbled on her earlobe, licked into her ear. "Good girl," he murmured. "Very good girl."

Warmth filled her chest. It never had been so easy to feel *right* as it was with these two brothers. She just hoped it was the same with the girls.

~.~

GAV'N CLEANED between Mira's legs with a washcloth, turning it into an inspection and spanking her when she tried to refuse his ministrations. He tidied her just in time because Jakk arrived shortly after with the girls in tow.

Their rashes had improved since they'd been at their grandparents, but their moods had not. Gav'n and Jakk had explained about Mira before they left, and they hadn't liked the idea. It seemed time away hadn't improved their opinions.

"Girls, this is Mira, our new permanent, live-in nanny. She's going to take care of you."

Pritzi, the youngest, stared at Mira with huge brown eyes and promptly burst into tears.

Horror flamed over Mira's face. "Hey, it's okay," she coaxed, "I know I'm ugly, but I'm not scary at all, I promise."

Darley's lips closed into a thin line, and she refused to say hello, even when both Gav'n and Jakk gave her their most stern looks. Jan, the middle child, didn't say a word, which they'd expected, since she hadn't spoken since their mother died.

Mira held her hand out to Pritzi, who eyed it suspiciously.

"You're not ugly," Pritzi said, her tears subsiding. She didn't take Mira's hand, though. "I like your hair."

Mira smiled. "I like yours, too. If you want, I can braid it tomorrow. I can make a whole crown around the top of your head."

The girl's eyes widened. She sniffed. "Out of hair?"

Mira nodded and tried offering her hand again. "Do you know what a braid is? When you weave the hair?"

Pritzi nodded, looking only half-certain she understood.

"I can make two braids. Or a fishtail. I had four sisters, so they taught me all kinds of things to do with hair."

"What's a fishtail?" Pritzi took her hand, now, and Mira led her into the girls' bedroom. Jan followed, but Darley remained in the living room, her arms crossed over her chest.

"Go on. Get ready for bed." Jakk had never been the warm, fuzzy type with the girls, and the strain between he and their surliest niece, Darley, in particular, had grown over the past few weeks.

"It's not my bedtime yet."

They'd gone easy on discipline. The girls had lost their mother, and their lives had been turned on end, but it was hard not want to come down on Darley when she started with the back talk. "It's your bedtime if we say it is," Jakk said evenly. "Go, now, or we'll permanently move bedtime up by a half hour."

Darley threw a baleful glance his way but flounced off to the bedroom.

Gav'n hesitated, torn between following to make sure Mira was okay in there, and giving them space. He opted for space but was reluctant to leave the living room where he could hear everything going on in the bedroom.

Jakk came to stand beside him, arms folded over his chest. The sound of Darley snarling at one of her sisters—*that's not yours, now put it down!*—sailed out of the room. Jakk flinched.

Gav'n knew his brother was as itchy as he was to solve the problem. But neither of them had been very successful at winning the girls' affection or obedience yet. They probably wouldn't do much better than Mira.

"Come on." Jakk bumped his shoulder. "She has to figure it out on her own."

Reluctantly, he peeled himself away from the room.

"I'm going to leave instructions for meals and chores for tomorrow," Jakk said, heading to the kitchen. "What did you decide to do about the collar?"

"I will weld it shut. It means we'll have to break it when we remove it, but at least it will work for the time being. I'll get some more at work. It's the adolescent size. It's not ideal, but it will get us through these first few weeks while we feel each other out."

He helped his brother by pulling out an electronic communication pad/translation device and listing the times things would happen during the day. He wrote in Pra'kirian and it translated his words into the foreign letters it said belonged to inhabitants of Earth. He added the times for leaving and picking up from school, even though the girls wouldn't be able to return until their rash went away. For chores, he started a list of the basics— washing clothes, scrubbing the bathrooms, cleaning the floors, shaking out rugs, etc.

Jakk planned meals and added the directions to the communication pad. Then they both crept back and peeked into the bedroom.

Darley sat in her bed, arms folded sulkily across her chest.

Mira lay beside Pritzi on the child's bed, not touching her, arms folded behind her head. "And when Harry received his invitation to Hogwarts, he didn't know anything about his parents being magic. He thought they'd died in a car accident..." Mira's voice had a singsong quality as she told a story of some kind.

Jan had her usual withdrawn expression, but she lay facing Pritzi's bed, eyes on Mira as she spoke.

He backed out before they saw him. Not bad for an introduction. It definitely could've been worse. Clearly, Mira had a knack with children.

He just hoped she could work a miracle with these particular children.

6

Mira shrieked and cursed as smoke billowed from the dryer. She threw open the door and waved the black plumes away enough to see inside. *Fuck.* Not a clothes dryer. What the hell was it?

Hearing the snicker of laughter behind her, she whirled and glared at Darley. "This isn't a clothes dryer, is it?"

The girl had the audacity to cover her mouth and giggle. Jan stood behind her, wide-eyed, and Pritzi shrieked, "Fire!"

"Yeah, I know it's a fire," she snapped. "Your sister told me this was a clothes dryer. What is it?" She looked to Jan, but the girl didn't speak. Jakk and Gav'n said she hadn't spoken since the day her mother died—poor child.

Pritzi crept closer and peered in. "It's where mama cooked meat."

Great. An oven of some sort. Why wasn't it in the kitchen?

"Well how do you dry your clothes?"

Darley sneered at the burning cloth. "I don't think they need drying now."

She drew a deep breath and counted to ten. It was hard not to dislike the girl. For starters, she appeared full-grown—to Mira, anyway. She was nearly the same height and probably weighed more than Mira. It made it easy to expect more from her, as if she were an adult. At least something about Darley's face still looked childlike—it helped Mira remember Darley was the equivalent of an eleven-year-old on Earth. Just a tween. One who'd recently lost her mom and surely blamed Mira for it.

"Darley, go to your room and don't come out until I say."

Apparently that wasn't a punishment on Pra'kir, because the girl smiled. "Okay," she said brightly and trotted off. The sound of her entertainment screen turned up loud came filtering back.

Great. She probably was supposed to have limited how much time they watched screens, too. She'd already let them watch them all morning. Getting their rashes cleared up so they could go to school had moved to her highest priority.

She huffed and yanked the singed clothing out of the contraption, dropping the items on the floor when they burned her fingers.

Jan moved in to help, but Mira threw out her arm to hold her back. "Careful, they're too hot." The girl's blank expression killed her. "Thank you, though."

Pritzi said, "I don't think we have a clothes dryer, Mira."

She sighed. "Where and how do you dry your clothes?"

Pritzi grasped her hand and led her to the washing machine. Mira looked around, trying to figure out where the dryer could be. Pritzi pointed at the washer. "This."

"This is the washing machine, Pritzi. Where do the clothes get dried?"

Pritzi tapped the machine. "In here."

She narrowed her eyes at the controls, which of course she couldn't read. Remembering the electronic pad with translated instructions the brothers had left, she went in search of it. Of course, she didn't know how it worked, and with her luck that day, would probably lose the screen with all their notes to her. Even so, she shifted it around, punching buttons until she managed to take a picture of the control panel.

Bingo!

It rearranged the characters into English. Sure enough, the

machine had a "dry" setting. Now, she knew. Too bad, like Darley had said, it was too late for the load she'd already incinerated. Those clothes wouldn't ever need drying again. But, at least, she'd figured something out on her own.

It seemed being a Pra'kirian housewife was harder than she'd thought.

Breakfast and lunch had been a semi-fiasco. Darley had given her misinformation on how to use what she thought was a microwave but actually was more like a convection oven. Which she had shorted out by turning it up too high with too much inside it. She now had the machine disassembled and in pieces all over the counter as she tried to diagnose the exact problem so she could fix it.

It also meant she'd burned their morning cereal. Fortunately, the girls seemed happy to eat some bright-red berries they'd produced— from where, she hadn't seen. Darley had even been nice enough to put some on a plate for her to try. They'd tasted sour to her, but the girls seemed to like them, and she wanted to show appreciation for their efforts, so she'd eaten all of them.

Now, though, her belly grumbled as if it hadn't appreciated the fruit. Which was too bad, because she'd been hoping by sticking mostly to fruit she would be indigestion-free. Looked like she'd be skipping dinner. She sure hoped the guys weren't going to be as intense as the guard at the prison over her eating habits.

She glanced down to see her two little shadows were still there, watching her every move. Putting them to bed the night before had been interesting. Darley was impossible, but the two younger girls let her tell them a bedtime story. When she realized they didn't know any of her childhood stories, she'd happily launched into the retelling of one of her favorite ancient book series. She figured she could go for years, retelling the stories she remembered. Pritzi had dropped off to sleep within a few minutes, but Jan had still been listening, so she went on a little longer for her before tucking her in.

She didn't have little brothers or sisters. She'd never babysat, or even wanted her own children. But she felt responsible for these little girls. Her ship killed their mom. As uncomfortable as caring for them was, she owed it to them to try her best.

She picked up Jan's arm and examined her hives. "Are these getting worse today?"

The mysterious rashes. The brothers had told her the doctors couldn't diagnose them and the academy wouldn't allow them to return until they'd cleared up.

She brushed the pad of her finger over one of the blisters. "Does it hurt? This really seems like some kind of allergy to me."

"What's allergy?" Pritzi asked.

"It's when your body has a reaction to something. Like a poison."

Jan's face blanched.

"Do you have that here?" She asked Jan the question, even though the girl wouldn't answer. She figured it was better to keep assuming one of these days she would open her mouth and speak again, rather than to cut her out of all conversations.

"Yes, we have poison," Pritzi said. "It's not poison, though, is it Jan?" she turned to her sister.

"I didn't mean you'd been poisoned. An allergy is not usually fatal, although it can be."

She glanced at the timepiece on the communication device. *Shit.* It was past time to start dinner preparation, according to their instructions.

She rushed to the kitchen, but it was still a complete disaster, the convection oven parts covering every inch of the countertop. She wouldn't be able to cook until she repaired the oven.

Of course, that was the moment Gav'n walked in. He stared across the living room and into the cramped kitchen she was hurriedly throwing parts into the hole that used to be the oven. "What in the hell happened here?"

She wiped at a black smudge on her nose she could see in her peripheral vision, but only seemed to make it larger. "I'm trying to burn the fucking house down. What does it look like to you?" she snapped. Defensiveness had always been her default mechanism for failure.

Gav'n stalked into the kitchen, eyes sweeping over the mess and the children. He stepped into her personal space, gripped the back of her hair, and yanked her head back. He claimed her mouth with a swift, dominant kiss and then murmured in a voice too low for the children to hear, "I'll be whipping that sass out of you shortly. Let me hear a *sorry, Master*." His deep, seductive voice contrasted with the tight pull on her scalp.

Heat flooded her core, and her irritability morphed into something more vulnerable. Even though she was clothed today, she felt as bared to Gav'n as ever. How did these aliens have the capacity to reduce her to a trembling mass of Jello?

He tugged a little harder when she didn't answer immediately.

"Yes, Master," she whispered.

A slow smile lit his face, and he eased the grip on her hair to massage her scalp instead. Her knees went weak.

But she sensed the stares of all three children—Darley had emerged from her room to watch the show as well.

"What happened here?" He still spoke low, in the sexy voice that belonged more in the bedroom than in an examination of her misdeeds as a nanny.

"I, uh, had a few accidents today."

His eyes flicked over the kitchen again. The corners of his lips twitched.

She shoved against his chest in irritation, but he caught her hand and brought it to his lips, kissing her fingers.

"And then you took things apart because the engineer in you wanted to see how they work?" He grinned like he found her absolutely charming, instead of a bumbling pain in the ass, like her family always had.

"Yes, Master."

He released her and moved into the kitchen, swiftly pulling things out of the chiller and assembling them on plates.

Jakk's steps sounded outside. Gav'n gripped her waist and propelled her toward the door. "Go greet your master with a kiss, *pashika*." He gave her a nudge.

She stumbled forward, tossing a quizzical look over her shoulder at Gav'n, who shooed her forward. She remembered Jakk's wooden explanation about why he'd never have a Pra'kirian mate. Did Gav'n hope she'd make up for it?

It was no less than she'd hoped when she'd given him that blow job, yet, for some reason, it bothered her. Jakk deserved more than a pity fuck. She genuinely found him attractive. Gav'n didn't need to urge her to make Jakk feel better about himself.

Like in the shuttle the day before, her anger with Pra'kirian women made her bold. She twined her arms around Jakk's neck the moment he walked in the door. "Welcome, Master."

He went rigid, as if unsure how to handle affection. She started to pull away, but his arm snaked around her waist and he pulled her up against his huge, hard body. "Hello little human. How did it go?"

He peered past her at the disaster in the kitchen and stiffened. When his gaze returned, he wore his more customary stern expression...which she seemed to find sexy.

Her nipples tightened against his body as his masculine scent filled her nostrils. Their faces were inches from each other, and the way he studied her made her feel beautiful. "Terrible," she answered honestly.

All day long, she truly had cursed them. She'd rehearsed a litany of complaints she planned to hurl at them, even knowing it would get her punished for disrespect. But they'd both disarmed her simply with—what? Their razor-sharp attention? Was that all it took to win her allegiance? Was she so attention-starved she would take anything from them—all forms of punishment and degradation, so long as they looked at her like she was their entire universe?

Maybe.

Yes.

Feeling all three girls' eyes on them, she pushed away. Darley's face was contorted with fury. Jan wore worry. Even Pritzi stared, somewhat dumbfounded.

"Are you going to mate Uncle Jakk or Uncle Gav'n?" the child asked.

Jakk stiffened against her, and she froze, too. Looking to him didn't help, either, because his face had closed off like shutters had been drawn. She darted a glance at Gav'n, who wore a furrow of concern between his brow.

"We're all family now. All six of us," she said.

The tension on Gav'n's face eased.

"I know none of us chose each other, but families are like that. You get stuck with who you get stuck with, and you make the best of it. That's how it works. I had four older sisters always telling me what to do or what I'd done wrong. Sometimes I hated it. But I also loved them." She choked a little at the end. Four sisters she'd never see again.

Jakk yanked her against his body roughly, squeezing the breath right out of her.

Darley still looked like she wanted to break something.

Too bad. They were stuck with each other.

~.~

JAKK GAZED down at Mira naked and bound spread-eagle to their bed. He'd been particularly ruthless that night. After what she'd said about them being a family—her miraculous acceptance of his most fervent desires, he had too much passion in him to be gentle. And with him, as with Gav'n, the urge to fuck also came with the urge to dominate. And so they'd tortured her, slapping and smarting every inch of her body as she writhed and squirmed on the bed, bringing her to the edge of orgasm over and over again until he finally pounded into her pussy while Gav'n fucked her mouth.

They'd had to spank it out of her, but she eventually confessed all her difficulties that day. They'd agreed to punish Darley by removing all screens for the following day.

"You do realize you're only making my life more difficult with that punishment?" Mira had complained, which they had answered with more spanking.

Now, Jakk released her and picked her up. "Let's get you in the shower, little one," he murmured, carrying her to the bathroom. He turned on the water and carried her right into the stall, not willing to set her down.

Possibly ever.

He wished he could take the collar off her for the night, but it was welded on now, and removing it would break the expensive piece of equipment. Fortunately, it was waterproof.

Water ran over her breasts, beading up on her pale skin, washing away his and Gav'n's scent. Gav'n pushed his way in, squeezing to the back of the shower. Gav'n lifted Mira's legs over his shoulders, tugging them open and bringing her juicy pussy to his mouth.

Jakk groaned, watching his twin flick his tongue over her clit, riling her up again.

"No more," she cried, voice raspy. "Please."

"I love it when she begs, don't you?" Gav'n flashed his cocky grin.

"Mmm, more than anything." Jakk balanced her back against his chest, pinching her nipples.

"No more...I can't...oh God, *yes*!" Her throaty cry made his cock rock-hard again.

"Should we let her come again, Gav'n?"

His brother sucked her clit, and she tore at his hair, desperate for release. "I don't know...she did burn our clothes up."

"I told you...that wasn't my...fucking...faul—ung, oh! Please, Jakk, Gav'n, Masters. Please!"

"She might need a proper whipping. I think when she uses the word *fuck* that way, it's a curse. Or a show of disrespect. And she ought to have learned to respect us by now."

Gav'n met his eyes as he went in for the kill, flicking his tongue fast over and over again until she screamed and came, quaking and shuddering.

Jakk shifted her torso to Gav'n's care, and his brother maneuvered her legs around his waist, her head collapsed over his shoulder. Their poor girl was wrung out with overuse. He stroked her wet head. "You're a good girl, Mira. Always available to your masters."

She let out a half-whine, half-sigh.

Jakk climbed from the shower and dried himself quickly then held a towel for their girl. Gav'n turned off the water and stepped out with her, transferring her into his arms and the waiting towel.

"I can dry myself off, you know," she mumbled, blushing.

"If your master wants to see to your care, you yield and say thank you, Master," Jakk said.

"Thank you, Master." Her surrender came easier each time. She had begun to trust them. "I know it's late, but do you think I could take a walk outside? I haven't left the house all day."

"No," Jakk said immediately.

Tension returned to her limp muscles, firming her slender body as she struggled for autonomy. "Why not?"

Gav'n flicked a towel across his back and raised one eyebrow. "We don't need a reason for setting rules, Mira. It's not your place to question them."

That made her frown. She wriggled, and he had to tighten his hold to keep her in his arms.

"I don't think she's been punished enough, tonight," Gav'n observed coolly.

It was part of her conditioning, Jakk knew, but it caused him physical pain to see her upset and to deny her anything she'd asked for. He *had* to explain. "It will cause the public distress to see you walking down the street after the way the footage of your crash has been playing over and over again. Someday, maybe, but not tonight, and never alone."

Her big blue-green eyes pleaded with him. "Not alone, then. With you both. It's dark. No one will see me."

His resolve slipped under her beautiful pleading gaze. Against his will, he flicked his eyes to Gav'n, who shrugged.

He sighed. "Shortest walk of your life. I'll take you. Someone has to stay with the girls in case they wake up."

"And that someone is me," Gav'n said.

Against his better instincts, he set her down and allowed her to dress while he threw on some clothes. Then he grasped her smaller hand in his own and led her down the stairs and out the door. They took the stairs down to the street and walked in silence through the back alleyway. He liked the feel of her hand nestled in his own, the sense of protectiveness she inspired in him. He'd never had a female to protect before. It was a wonderful responsibility.

"If you and Gav'n weren't so...um...*attentive* to me, I would be freaking right now."

He furrowed his brow at the words that hadn't translated. "What is freaking?"

"Worried sick. Upset."

He stopped and spun her to face him, catching her up in his arms. "About what?"

Her slender hands came to his chest but she didn't push with any real intent. "Everything. Living here with you, raising the girls. Trying to integrate on a planet I know nothing about."

His stomach dropped for her. He wrapped her head up against his chest and kissed the top of it. "I'm so sorry, little one. It must be terrifying for you. Tell me you're not afraid of me...of Gav'n?" He held his breath, waiting for her reply. He supposed he should want her afraid, for the conditioning, but, at this moment, her trust meant far more.

She shook her head. "Not really...sometimes a bit. But I'm beginning to understand you both. You don't mean me harm, even if we don't see eye to eye on how I should be treated."

He arched a brow. "Don't we?"

Under the light of three full moons, her face glowed pale, but he thought her cheeks colored.

"I think you rather enjoy the way we treat you. Even when it involves stern discipline."

Yes, definitely a flush.

He cupped her chin. "Say it."

She tried to pull away but he wouldn't allow it. "Say what?"

"Say you like when we punish you."

She colored even darker. "No way—I don't."

"I've touched your pussy after punishment. You're always wet for us. You love your spankings. Say it."

She tried once more to squirm out of his grasp, and when she realized she couldn't, she whined, "Jakk."

"Say it, or next time you won't be rewarded after you're punished."

Her lips set in a firm line.

"Is that your choice?"

A lift of her chin.

"So be it."

He released her and tugged her forward, resuming the walk.

She jogged to catch up with his longer stride. "I-I might like some aspects." She sounded breathless.

He smirked, but no sense of superiority arrived. In fact, something about this delicate human, the ward whose entire life he controlled, always left him humbled. Earning her trust, seeing the resistance ebb away and the glow of warmth start to simmer in those ocean-green eyes made his entire existence spin on its head. He may control her life, but she certainly had plucked the strings of his heart. Of course, he knew he could never expect her to feel real love for him —an unfit male—but at least she might come to accept him.

~.~

It felt incredible to be outside. After the weeks in prison and now cooped up in the house, fresh air—especially the sea air—healed her with every breath. Unfortunately, their walk was all too short. They looped around the block, and Jakk led her back toward the house.

In the street, they passed the next door neighbor, a stooped, elderly woman who stopped her mopping—yes, she was *mopping* the porch!—and openly stared at Mira as they walked by.

"That's one of the alien invaders. They moved her in next door."

The being crouched on the step behind her spoke as if they couldn't hear. It was not a Pra'kirian, at least not the same species as Gav'n and Jakk. It resembled a naked sloth.

"Good evening, Linat, Arnc," Jakk said coldly. He tugged her elbow and led her away, into their tiny yard.

"Um, what was that?" she whispered when they'd passed.

"He's a Mekron. About twenty years ago, we launched a manned expedition to one of the moons, the biggest discovery of which was an alien ship we found drifting, powerless, in our debris belt. No one knew how sick they were until we brought them home, fostered them out—much like we did you—and they'd been with us a while."

"Sick?" she echoed.

"The first began to show symptoms six months after they arrived. A strange... rash that wouldn't go away."

The girls. She peered up at him, but he looked steadfast at their feet and just kept walking.

"Eventually, the rash became... I don't know, it's some kind of mummifying disease, one that causes fungus-like growths to eat their bodies from the inside out." He was quiet a few steps more before softly admitting, "The first died five years later, and they've been dying ever since. And it all started with a rash our doctors can't quite figure out." Even more softly a few steps later, he said, "That's why we can't keep a nanny, and that's why their school doesn't want the girls there. Whatever is killing the Mekron, they think it's finally jumped species."

"Oh." A sick feeling twisted in her gut. She hoped to God the girls' rash wasn't related.

She stopped to pluck a bright-red berry from one of the bushes in the yard.

Jakk knocked it out of her fingers when she brought it to her mouth. "What are you doing? Those aren't edible."

She picked another one, examining it. "They aren't?" Nibbling the tiniest bit of its skin, she sampled it. "They look and taste exactly like the berries the girls had for breakfast. What were those?"

He stared. "What berries?"

"They were just like these. The girls ate them for breakfast and gave me a plate, too."

Jakk's expression turned grim, and he pounded up the stairs and threw open the door.

"Shh." She raced up behind him. "Jakk, you'll wake the girls."

"I plan to," he growled, stalking into their bedroom and switching on the light. "Wake up, girls. We need to have a talk."

Gav'n jogged down the stairs and joined them. "What's going on?"

The girls sat up, rubbing their eyes and blinking at the light.

"Mira says the girls ate the berries from the bush outside for breakfast."

Pritzi burst into tears, and Jan turned pale. Even Darley shrank down into her covers at Jakk's booming voice.

"And you fed them to Mira, as well? Whose idea was this? Darley's?" He turned a furious gaze on the oldest girl. "So, the berries are the cause of the rash?"

"Are they?" Gav'n boomed when no one answered.

Mira couldn't take the sight of Pritzi backed into the corner of her bed, sobbing. She joined her there and scooped the small girl into her arms.

"You realize you could've killed yourselves? The body makes a rash to get the poison out. Your little sister could've died from this harebrained idea of yours. And all for what? Attention? To stay out of school? What is this about?"

Darley's face crumpled now.

"And you fed them to Mira? She's not even the same species. What if they were fatal to her?" Gav'n paced the room like an angry tiger.

Even Jakk's normally stiff expression lit with anger. "Your mother didn't believe in physical punishment, but maybe—"

"No," Mira interrupted. She had strong beliefs against corporal punishment for children, which had long ago been outlawed on Earth.

Jakk and Gav'n both looked at her in surprise. The girls did, too.

"That's not the solution," she said firmly, willing them to accept her opinion for once.

Jakk drew in a measured breath then exhaled. "One month with no screens, no excursions, no fun of any kind. You'll go to school tomorrow and explain what you've been up to and why you're safe to return. And if any of you misleads Mira on anything again—anything at all—I will make you all very sorry. Understood?"

"Yes, Uncle," Darley muttered, managing to appear surly, even through her tears. Jan sniffed and nodded, which was the most communication Mira had seen from her. Pritzi snuffled, "Yes, Uncle," her little chest heaving with sobs still. Mira rubbed her back and lowered her to her side, curling her body around the girl and petting her.

Jakk turned off the light, and he and Gav'n left the room.

Mira held her breath, listening to the three girls sniffling, her heart twisting in pain for them. They were troubled, certainly. Probably the sound scolding had been necessary, but she only wanted to soothe them. To promise them the pain of their mother's loss would ebb, in a year or two. That they would feel like participating in their lives again at some point, and that they were still loved.

But she didn't know them, and they hated her. So she settled for staying in their room until they fell asleep and creeping out with a heavy heart.

7

M ira held the communication/translator pad up to the screen on Jakk's intelligence device. She'd been working at it since the moment everyone left the house. Jakk had left early, and Gav'n had taken the girls to school to explain about the berries and convince them to allow the girls back in, despite the fact the rashes hadn't disappeared yet.

They'd left her a list of chores to do, and she was responsible for picking the girls up, but her priority was figuring out where her shipmates had been placed. So far, she'd spent over an hour just figuring out how to navigate Jakk's device.

There was no news service report about any of their placements, other than the brief news of the Council's decision to foster them out.

Where were her friends? What had happened to them? Were they being "conditioned" by the same methods she was?

Her back and neck had grown stiff from leaning over for so many hours. She sighed and stood, rolling her shoulders. She had cooking and cleaning to do, and the stupid oven still needed to be repaired. She found Jakk's little music device and switched it on. Ugh. The music was awful, although she understood Jakk found it beautiful. It reminded her of listening to music of other cultures back on Earth. Some sounded screechy and disharmonious to her ears.

It was strange that there were no speakers for the unit. She guessed they hadn't invented surround sound on Pra'kir. Maybe they heard things differently. Their sense of smell seemed keener than hers. They always claimed to know she was aroused by her scent.

She hurriedly cleaned the bathrooms and floors then finished disassembling the stove until she found the fried heating coil and thermocouple. She placed them on the table to ask one of the men to order, or—her preference—to show her how to order things. Would they give her an expense account? For some reason, the thought made her giggle.

The old-fashioned kept-woman thing titillated her on some level. She had fantasies of greeting the men naked and giving them each a blowjob to ask for money. But the fantasies were only appealing in a pretend world. Not having her own bank account or funds wasn't cute in real life. She needed a real job, an income, freedom.

Fuck.

Would she ever find happiness and fulfillment on Pra'kir? Sexually, she had. But there was more to life than sex. And no matter how kind her masters were to her, no matter how attentive, they couldn't make up for the fact that she would be living as a child for the rest of her life.

~.~

MIRA SET the shuttle program for the school, thrilled to be out of the townhouse. These twice-daily trips had become her only excursions, only ventures into fresh air. Gav'n and Jakk had promised they'd take her somewhere soon, but it had been two weeks of monotony. She almost wished the girls were still home with their rashes during the day.

She could chisel the damn shock collar off if she needed to, but it was better to bide her time and build trust. After she found the location of her shipmates, she'd get rid of the collar to slip away undetected for at least a visit.

The shuttle drove itself straight to the academy and pulled into the circular drive. The girls stood out front, waiting. Mira was under strict orders not to leave the shuttle for any reason. Gav'n said it would be bad enough if anyone spotted her inside the vehicle, but if they saw her outside, there might be trouble.

The girls jumped into the shuttle quickly, like they were embarrassed to be seen with her. She gunned the shuttle, and it charged back down the tracks to the main speedway, moving automatically.

"How was your day, girls?"

No one answered.

"Pritzi?"

She glanced in the rear-view mirror. The little girl looked exhausted. She seemed too young to be in school. On Earth, she'd only be in preschool.

All three girls had circles under their eyes and somber faces. What had they liked to do before their mother died? What would she want, if she were in their shoes?

She'd want to be out in nature on a hike or simply in fresh air. She gazed out the window at the scenery whizzing by. The coastal city of Endermere was absolutely breathtaking. She still longed to go to the beach. In the other direction, lay hills.

On a whim, she overrode the programming in the shuttle and took the exit off the speedway toward the hills. A little fresh air was exactly what these girls needed.

Darley noticed first. She sat up taller and looked out the window. "Where are we going?"

The slight note of alarm in her voice made Mira smile.

"I thought we'd go pick some wildflowers."

"What?"

"How do we do that?" Pritzi asked.

"Well, I'm not sure. I'm finding a good place to pull off so we can go exploring."

Pritzi started bouncing in her seat. "Really? We get to go exploring? *Whooshka!*"

She followed the road and took another turn, down a set of tracks that bumped and jolted the shuttle like they were old and out of repair. She followed it until she saw a turnabout and stopped the shuttle. "Let's get out."

"Here?" Darley asked doubtfully.

"Yes, here. Why not?"

"Is this someone's property?"

Mira shrugged and climbed out of the shuttle. "Probably, but I don't see anyone around. Come on, girls. We won't stay long. Just enough time to pick some flowers. Look at them all!" The hills were dotted with color—yellows, purples, blues, reds. Giant butterflies skimmed the tops of the fragrant blossoms, adding to the rainbow of color.

Pritzi and Jan threw their doors open and climbed out. Darley followed a moment later.

Mira stooped and picked a fistful of purple flowers, leaving the stems long enough to weave together. She started braiding them, walking slowly and picking other colors as she ambled toward the hills.

Pritzi ran up beside her. "What are you doing?"

"Making you a flower wreath. Want to help?"

"What's a wreath?"

"A crown. Ooh, see those yellow flowers over there? Get me some."

Pritzi raced to help, gathering handfuls of flowers and racing back with them. "Mira, look at this one! Do you want white?"

"Yes, baby. I want every color. Pick me the whole stem—like this, see?" She held up the stems in her hand to show how long she needed them.

Jan joined the picking frenzy. Only Darley refused, arms folded, kicking at the flowers with her human adult-sized feet.

Mira found a flat rock and settled on it to weave a crown for each girl. Pritzi ran back and forth, bringing her new blossoms and watching wide-eyed as she created the wreaths. Jan, too, brought flowers, although she didn't make eye contact when she surreptitiously set them beside Mira.

When she finished all three, she made a fake trumpeting sound with her fist up to her mouth. "Pritzi, I crown thee Princess of Endermere." She placed the largest wreath on Pritzi's head.

"What's a princess?"

Of course, the girls didn't know what princess or royalty meant.

"It's being a ruler. But it's better than the Council of Nine. It's more like being the most beautiful, pure, *and* powerful in all the land."

"Oh, it's like the premier," Pritzi said.

Mira dropped a crown on Jan's head. "Jan, I crown thee Princess Premier of Endermere."

Jan didn't smile, but Mira thought she liked it, nonetheless.

She drew a breath and regarded Darley. "And Darley, I crown thee—"

"I don't want your stupid crown."

"You're mean, Darley," Pritzi shouted. She took the wreath from Mira in her little chubby hand. "You wear it, Mira." She stood on her tiptoes, as if she might reach.

Mira dropped to one knee to let Pritzi crown her. "Okay, girls. I guess we'd better get back before your uncles realize I've broken all the rules."

"Too late," Darley muttered.

The bright yellow and red police shuttle hurtled down the tracks toward them.

She stood and hastened toward their shuttle, not wanting to run into anyone. "Come on, girls. Get in the shuttle."

"It's Uncle Gav'n," Pritzi announced, pointing. "See?"

She nibbled her lip, her belly flip-flopping. She'd known they'd see she deviated from instructions, but she hadn't been sure how they'd react. It seemed she was about to find out.

~.~

HEART IN HIS THROAT, Gav'n threw open the door of his police shuttle and charged out. And then stopped. A thousand scenarios had flashed through his mind when he'd seen Mira go rogue, but this wasn't one of them.

His nieces skipped down the hill with Mira wearing crowns of— were they flowers? A huge smile stretched across Pritzi's face, and Jan's eyes shone bright, her cheeks flushed pink with fresh air and exertion. Even Darley's scowl didn't diminish the pretty sight they made.

He put his hands on his hips and waited for them to arrive.

"Uncle Gav'n, I'm a princess," Pritzi chirped. She looked so precious with the flower wreath, he couldn't help but scoop her up into his arms and blow a raspberry against her neck like he used to before her mom died. When all he had to be was the fun uncle who visited and brought them trinkets.

She shrieked and giggled, her little hands flying up to push his face away.

He set her down and fixed Mira with a condemning stare. It was hard to be angry, though, when she radiated beauty, so refreshed, so *happy*.

Something twisted in his gut. Was she that unhappy normally? Maybe he and Jakk had been fooling themselves into believing she might grow comfortable with them. When she pulled unexpected stunts like these, it served as a reminder she very much still kept her own counsel and didn't fear their punishments nearly enough.

They'd been too soft on her, ending every punishment in pleasure. But he couldn't imagine not letting her see how much they adored her.

"I know you're mad," she said softly. "I wasn't running away, if that's what you thought. Or stealing your children."

The fact she knew where his mind had gone served as another reminder. Their girl was smart.

He pursed his lips. "Come here, Mira."

Her face flushed as she stepped forward, bringing her body close enough for her intoxicating scent to reach his nostrils.

He gripped her arms and lowered his face to hers. "You are in a big trouble, little human," he growled, keeping his voice down for the sake of his nieces.

"I know." She sounded so matter-of-fact. This had been a calculated move on her part. She chose to disobey because she thought the reward outweighed the punishment.

And it looked like it had. Yes, terrible things might have happened. The owner of this property could've arrived and called the police or worse—taken the law into his own hands. But nothing bad had happened. She'd succeeded in bonding a little more with the girls, which was sorely needed.

He leaned closer, bringing his face inches from hers. "Tonight, little girl," he warned in a low voice, "I fuck your ass."

Her eyes flew wide, lips parted. To his delight, her pupils dilated, and he knew, from the hectic color flushing her face, he'd excited her.

He turned her toward the shuttle and slapped her ass, hard. "Get in the shuttle and get yourselves home. I'll deal with your misbehavior later."

The look she shot over her shoulder made his cock rock-hard. Fear mingled with excitement. His favorite combination.

~.~

MIRA COULDN'T EXTINGUISH the buzzing in her body. Gav'n was going to punish her by fucking her ass. His cock was way too big. Yes, they'd used a plug on her, even a vibrating plug, but that was different from a huge alien cock.

Heat pooled in her core, feathered across her skin.

She'd like to say she hated when they punished her anally, but it wasn't true. As humiliating as it was to have her ass fucked with a plug or vibrator, it felt so. Damn. Good. Especially when they gave her vaginal penetration at the same time.

Oh God. *Double penetration.* Would they actually make her take *two cocks at once?*

Her pulse fluttered as she finished putting the dinner dishes away and headed into the girls' room to put them to bed.

She'd worked her ass off when she got home to get dinner ready on time, even setting the table with the wildflowers from her wreath.

Neither Gav'n nor Jakk had said anything to her, but the tension had been there. The knowledge she was in trouble and she'd be answering to them soon hung so thick she swore she could see it shimmering in the air between them.

She kept the bedtime story short that night, unable to concentrate. "All right, girls, lights out," she said, getting up.

"Are you in big trouble, Mira?" Pritzi asked in a hushed voice.

"Yes," she sighed. "I'm in trouble."

"What will they do to you?" All three girls waited for her answer.

"I'm sure they'll punish me. Don't worry about it, baby." She ruffled the child's hair and gave her forehead a kiss.

She hesitated, wanting to do the same for the older girls. No, they'd rebuff her. Someday, maybe, they'd let her cuddle them the way she wanted to.

The door closed behind her with a snap. To stall, she did another sweep of the downstairs, but everything was in its place, all dishes put away and surfaces wiped down. Nothing to do but go upstairs.

Her clit pulsed as she took the stairs, heart hammering. She pushed open the door. Gav'n lounged on the bed. Jakk sat on the sofa, reading and listening to his awful music. He closed his book and set it down.

There was no mistaking the wicked intent in both of their faces.

"Clothes off." Gav'n's cool command sent a shiver down her spine.

She unhooked the jumper and pulled it off. They still hadn't permitted her to wear underclothing, so she stood naked. Her nipples beaded. She wasn't sure which one of them to face, so she chose somewhere in the middle, folding her hands in front of her.

"You broke a rule today, Mira," Jakk said from the sofa. He'd looked stern all evening, and she'd worried about his displeasure. Were they truly angry? Or was this more of their usual funishment?

"If we can't trust you to follow our guidelines, we'll never be able to relax them. You do understand that, don't you?"

She pursed her lips. Arguing probably wasn't in her best interests, but she also didn't think she'd done anything wrong. If she weren't a prisoner, she'd be allowed to stop and pick flowers anytime she liked. And she still didn't think she deserved to be held as a prisoner.

There they differed.

"Come here, Mira. Your punishment will start with me." Jakk patted his thighs.

Fear fluttered in her belly, along with the thrill of lying over his lap. She remembered how the first time over his lap had ended, and it hadn't been all bad.

She walked to the sofa and knelt beside him, lying across his lap and lowering her torso onto the cushion.

He stroked her bare bottom with his huge hand. "Good girl. We like it when you obey." He gathered her wrists behind her back and pinned them there then trapped her legs under one of his.

She expected his palm, so when something as hard as wood crashed down on one cheek and then the other, she choked on a cry and craned her neck over her shoulder to see. Jakk had a small oval paddle—more narrow and thick than a Ping-Pong paddle—and it hurt like the devil. He wasn't going slow, either. He set up an even pace, striking one buttock then the other about every half second.

Panic erupted as the blaze set in, but as much as she struggled, she couldn't get free of Jakk's hold.

"Ow...ow, ow, ow," she wailed as he continued to beat her with the mean instrument. "That hurts. Oh my God, that hurts! Please...ow, Jakk—Master—don't. *Stop!*"

The horrible paddling stopped, and he rested his heavy hand with the implement on the back of her pelvis. "I don't think she's sorry yet, do you, Gav'n?"

"I know she's not."

"Wait—"

But Jakk had already renewed his rapid-fire assault on her squirming ass.

"Jakk—Gav'n—I'm sorry, I'm sorry. Stop!" Sobs choked her voice, or was it desperation? Every fight-or-flight instinct had been activated, but she couldn't get out of Jakk's grasp. Each time the paddle struck, it set off a new burst of flames, and she was sure she couldn't survive one more swat.

Jakk stopped again, and she collapsed over his legs, catching her breath. "I think she does whatever she wants to do, regardless of what rules we set. Is that how you see it, Gav'n?"

"No!" she shouted because he'd picked up the implement hand again. "Wait! Stop!"

Jakk began another volley of spanks, smarting her poor throbbing ass, which had to already be swollen and red from the terrible paddle.

"You're hurting me," she wailed, although that obviously was the point. Still, this time seemed so long and severe. So relentless. It definitely wasn't funishment.

"If you wanted to go and pick flowers, you should have asked our permission. Would that be so hard, naughty girl?"

Asking their permission hadn't really occurred to her, since she'd assumed everything she wanted was against the rules, anyway.

"Would you have let me?" she demanded then immediately wished she hadn't because Jakk picked up the intensity. "Ow! I'm sorry! I'm sorry! Master, please. No-more-I'm-so-sorry!"

Jakk stopped again, resting the smooth wood of the paddle against her twitching, screaming cheeks.

"I'm sorry," she moaned, collapsing again. Real tears choked her voice. "Please don't spank me anymore. I've learned my lesson."

"Have you?" Jakk's voice cracked like a whip.

"Yes, Master. I will follow your rules," she sniffed. "Or ask permission to deviate."

Jakk didn't move, and she lifted her head to see Gav'n, certain they were communicating. Gav'n was nodding at Jakk.

She stiffened for another round, but Jakk's leg lifted from her thighs.

He slapped at the back of one thigh. "Open."

She parted without question.

"Wider," he barked. When his fingers found her pussy, his touch was rough, aggressive. "She's wet," he said with satisfaction.

Yes. Despite the harshness of the spanking, her pussy had moistened the moment she'd laid over Jakk's lap. In fact, it seemed the harder he paddled, the wetter she became.

"I told her no pleasure after her next punishment."

She jerked her head up. "But I admitted it! I told you I might like my spankings."

Despite his pronouncement, the tip of one finger was idly circling her clit, nearly making her weep with desire.

"I'm not inclined to give her pleasure," Gav'n said from the bed.

Jakk removed his touch.

"Not unless she begs for what we all know she deserves."

"An ass-fucking?" Jakk supplied.

Gav'n's eyes glittered. "Yes. Her ass-fucking. Maybe that will teach her who is in charge around here."

An itchiness spread through her, concentrating between her legs. Her throbbing ass didn't want to be touched, much less fucked, but it seemed the rest of her disagreed.

Jakk parted her cheeks and applied an oil. "I'll put the plug in until she's ready to admit what she needs."

Her pussy contracted on air. The quivering in her core hadn't stopped. The nose of the plug nudged her back entrance, and she unwittingly lifted her ass to take it.

"Did you see that?" Jakk's voice sounded thick.

"I saw." Gav'n, too, sounded excited.

She whined as the plug stretched her wide and then seated.

Jakk didn't let her adjust to it, though. Instead, he pumped it slowly, easing it in and out, driving her mad.

Her poor butt cheeks stung and burned, but she loved the sensation of being filled by the plug.

She fought for her hands, dying to touch her pussy.

"Our girl's getting needy." The deep timbre of Jakk's voice, the way he spoke about her with reverence, made her crazy for him, for more.

"Tell me what you need, little human," Gav'n demanded, his voice deep and rough.

"I need—" She arched her bottom toward Jakk, desperate for more, even if it was only anal stimulation. "Gav'n...Master...I need you to..." Her lips and tongue felt thick. She was afraid she would drool on the sofa.

In a flash, Gav'n was up off the bed, kneeling beside her face, pushing her hair back. "What do you need, *pashika*?"

She licked her lips. "Fuck me. Fuck my ass. Please, Master."

Her world tilted and swooped as both men moved at once. Jakk lifted and tipped her into Gav'n's arms, and he carried her to the bed, where he arranged her on her hands and knees. He pushed between her shoulder blades, lowering her torso until her face hit the bed.

"Spread those legs for me, little girl. Show me that naughty ass."

She didn't know how her knees held her up, but she widened her stance, presenting her ass in the most humiliating fashion possible.

Gav'n slapped her pussy. "Do you think we should touch you here, naughty girl?"

"Yes!" she gasped.

He slapped again, harder. "Like this?"

"No...yes." She wasn't sure what she wanted. She definitely needed her pussy touched, desperately. But *spanked* was another thing.

"I'll bet," Gav'n said, manipulating the plug in her ass, "if you do a really good job sucking Jakk's cock right now, he'll touch your pussy and make sure you're satisfied while I fuck your ass."

She pushed up to her hands, turning her head to seek Jakk.

~.~

JAKK'S COCK had hardened to blue-ball proportions, as often was the case around their little human. The way she sought him with her eyes now nearly made him growl aloud. Could she actually *want* to give him a blowjob?

She was the only female who ever had. But he supposed they had riled her up to the point of desperation.

"Good girl," Gav'n murmured, rewarding her with a brief swipe of her clit.

Jakk undid his pants and came over to the bed, sliding his large frame in front of her until his cock arrived in line with her face.

She lunged for it and wrestled his length from his pants.

Satisfaction surged as she lowered her lush mouth down over his length. "Mira," he choked, catching her hair in his fist and using it to lift and lower her head. "You are very good at that."

She hummed, sending the vibration straight through to his throbbing member. Her fist curled around the base of his cock, and she used her hand to follow her mouth, making it seem like she took all of it into her throat every time she lowered.

He groaned.

Gav'n generously oiled his cock. "Don't lose focus on my brother, Mira," he warned, "or we won't touch your pretty little pussy while I pound your ass."

Jakk saw genuine fear in her expression, and he stroked her cheek. "Don't worry, *pashika*. Gav'n knows what he's doing. You're safe with us."

She resumed sucking, her eyes locked on his face. Pleading for mercy? Or watching for his satisfaction? Either way, it brought him close to losing control. He thrust his hips, shoving his cock up into her throat, unable to hold back.

She didn't protest. Her free hand gripped his ass, fingernails digging into his skin as she moved in concert with his thrusts, squeezing his cock so wonderfully tight.

"That's it, Mira," he grunted.

Gav'n rubbed the head of his cock against her anus and, instead of protesting, she bobbed faster over Jakk's cock, as if eager to please.

Gav'n waited, watching.

He mentally thanked his brother for not interrupting this sacrosanct moment.

Mira sucked harder, cheeks hollowed, blue-green eyes wide and desperate, as if her own satisfaction rode on how well she blew him.

His thighs flexed; cum shot from his shaft. "Mira, yes," he shouted, stars dancing before his eyes.

She swallowed his seed, still sucking like her life depended on it.

His eyes burned. Had she really offered that so freely to him?

No, they'd made her feel obligated, that was all. Still, nothing could stop the surge of affection he experienced for their ward.

"*Pashika*," he murmured, extricating himself from her grasp and sliding around to where he could reach between her legs.

Slick with nectar.

His girl had liked sucking him off. Or was it Gav'n at her rear hole? Either way, he loved her so turned on. He stroked slowly along her slit, delighting in the satisfied shiver she gave.

Gav'n pushed at her anus, and she tensed.

Jakk found her clit and pinched it between two fingers.

Mira gasped, and Gav'n pressed the advantage, breaching her hole and easing inside her tight channel.

He fisted Mira's hair and turned her head to him, one cheek pressed to the bed. Her eyes were wide and frightened, fingers pulling at the covers.

"Open for Gav'n, *pashika*. When you're naughty, your ass belongs to us." It wasn't true. If she hadn't asked for it, Gav'n wouldn't have forced himself on her, but she didn't need to know that. The issue of her selective obedience needed to be met with consistence dominance and discipline.

Her sweet mouth opened, and a constricted mewl issued from her throat as Gav'n filled her ass with the whole of his cock.

Jakk worked a finger into her pussy, and she began to emit short, guttural sounds, like an animal in heat. "You like being filled by both of us, little one?"

"Ugn...ugn...oh!" she panted.

He loved her vocalizations. "Naughty girl. You disobeyed your masters today." He screwed his digit deeper.

"Sorry," she gasped. "I need...ugn!"

Gav'n slid in and out, and Jakk timed his finger-thrusts into her pussy on his brother's out-strokes.

"Please," she whined.

"Quiet, naughty girl. You don't get satisfaction until Gav'n's taken you long and hard."

Her pussy spasmed around his finger, and the knowledge his dominant talk had brought her to her first orgasm gave him pleasure. She did crave their mastery, no matter how much she protested.

Gav'n appeared close to the edge, though, so their sweet human wouldn't have to wait long. A sheen of sweat gathered on his forehead, probably from the effort of holding back. They'd discussed the danger of hurting her back hole if they were too rough.

"Bad, bad girl," Gav'n growled, shoving deep on each word. He gripped her hips to hold her pelvis in place as his flesh slapped into her red, chastised bottom.

"I'm sorry," she babbled. "I was bad...so bad...yes, fuck me hard...*oh Gawd!*"

Jakk found the raised tissue on the inside wall of her channel and rubbed it, making her scream and lose control, her muscles contracting around his finger again.

Gav'n's face contorted as his orgasm came on and he released her hips, forcing her to her belly with his last, orgasmic thrust.

Jakk wiggled his finger as the aftershocks ran through their girl flattened on the bed under his brother. Eyes closed, mouth open, hair tangled in a wild halo around her, she was the most beautiful thing he'd ever seen.

And she was theirs.

If only she would accept her place with them.

8

av'n answered his brother's communication call. They both were at work, and he'd been hoping he'd at least make it through the entire week without having to attend to some problem at home.

But that was probably too much to ask.

He accepted the call, bracing himself. "Hey, twin."

"She's been messing with my computer," Jakk said tersely.

"What do you mean? What did she do?"

"Research of some sort. It looks like she was searching for information on her own case."

His heart squeezed. "Do you think she found it?"

Jakk rubbed his forehead. "I don't know. I wish she'd asked us if she wanted more information. I don't like this."

He didn't tell his brother he had concerns of his own. He'd found a pile of parts in the outdoor shed, as if she were squirrelling away pieces of technology to build something. But what? A means of communicating with Earth, her home planet? Did she harbor the ambition of returning? He'd thought, from reading her file, she'd told the general magistrate it was impossible. But perhaps she'd lied. The humans' technology was more advanced than Pra'kir's. And their little human was the technology engineer. Perhaps their plan all along had been to build a device enabling them to contact their home planet. What if they brought on a full invasion? As police commissioner, he had an obligation to take action if he felt the human a danger to society. And yet, he couldn't bring himself to tell even Jakk, with whom he practically shared a mind.

The truth was, he was falling for Mira. And, while he knew she was Jakk's only chance for a mate, he couldn't reconcile himself to the idea of letting his brother have her exclusively. It would be the right thing to do. He could choose from any number of women in Endermere once Jakk and Mira were successfully mated and settled. But he didn't want to find another. He didn't want to ever leave the odd little family they'd formed.

But, of course, none of that mattered, if their little ward plotted to escape them, or, worse, leave the planet.

"Do you think we should limit her access to all communication devices?" Jakk sounded as unhappy about the suggestion as it made him feel.

She already chafed against the bounds they'd set for her. Further restrictions would only make her more dishonest. Because they both knew she'd seek a way around any limitations.

"Let's ask her," he suggested. "Ask what she wants to know and give her the information. I know it seems counterintuitive, but maybe if we offer more trust, she'll become trustworthy."

Jakk rubbed his forehead again. "Do you think she'll ever settle in with us? Or will she always be looking for a way out?"

The pain on his brother's face on the screen triggered a twinge of guilt. He shouldn't allow himself to think of Mira as his when she was the only woman Jakk could ever hope to have a relationship with. If they failed to condition and keep Mira, it would destroy Jakk. After a lifetime of being resigned to never having a female, Mira represented every hope and dream his brother never dared believe possible. To lose her or miss this chance would be beyond cruel.

"I think we need to show her she has no reason to run. Maybe we need to try harder to make her happy—beyond sex."

Jakk's expression remained bleak. "How?"

Indeed, how? The girls hadn't taken to her yet. And it wasn't as if raising children had been her life goal—it was one they'd chosen for her. No, she was an intelligent engineer who'd contributed to her own society in important ways. Ways Pra'kir might never allow. She might never be trusted by their society, nor given technology or tools to work with. The Council wanted her and her shipmates tucked safely away. But she was full of scientific information Pra'kir could put to good use. They'd be stupid not to give her a job where she could use her knowledge to advance Pra'kirian state of the art.

He scrubbed a hand across his jaw. "Maybe a trip to the beach? She loves being outdoors. Could you work your connections to find a private beach getaway? We couldn't bring her anywhere public."

Jakk's jaw firmed with resolve. "I'll figure something out. See you at home."

~.~

Mira parked the bullet shuttle in front of the food market on the way home from school and got out. "Let's go, girls."

Gav'n had told her to send Darley in for the few staples they needed, but she wanted to see what the market was like. She clutched the currency card Gav'n had left, feeling naked without a wallet or purse like she'd have on Earth.

Darley ducked her head, probably embarrassed about being seen with her and scooted on ahead. Pritzi held her hand, and Jan hung behind them a half-step.

Okay, maybe she didn't fit in as well as she thought. Every head swung around and the Pra'kirians pointed, openly gawking.

"That's one of the aliens," one woman said loudly.

A loud murmur of voices rose.

Someone held up a communication tablet, like they were taking pictures or filming her.

Fuck.

Part of her wanted to shove the currency card in Darley's hand, tell her what to get, and run for the shuttle. But the most stubborn part of her had to see this through. She lifted her chin and marched through the store. The fact she didn't know where to find anything made it infinitely worse, but she eventually grabbed the box of grain the Pra'kirians used for their morning cereal and headed to the counter. The rest could wait.

Her vision tunneled, and a din rose in her ears, which was good, because it blocked out all the voices talking about her. Heart thudding, she thunked the box of grain on the counter and held out the card.

The checkout person—a pimply faced girl—stared at her for a full four seconds before taking the card. Her lip curled as if Mira smelled bad.

She named the price and beeped the card, which Gav'n had explained served as an automatic debit system.

Mira grabbed the grain and the card, not waiting to see if there would be a receipt or a bag to put the box into. She marched out of the store, hoping to God the girls had followed because she couldn't bring herself to look right or left.

Outside, her nose began to burn.

Dear Lord, they hated her. If she'd thought the girls' reception of her presence had been bad, this had been a whole deeper level.

She dropped into the seat of the shuttle and started it, her vision fixed on the steering wheel without seeing. She waited until the two shuttle doors slammed, then she took off. No one said a word on the drive home.

Gav'n, however, met them at home, fury evident in the slash of his brows and the tightness of his mouth. "What did I tell you to do at the store? Did I say go inside?"

The news station was playing on the screen on the wall behind him, showing footage of her marching through the store.

Oh Lord. "No." She didn't want the girls to see her cry. She whirled and dashed back out the front door.

"You stop right there." Gav'n's voice sounded menacing, and she didn't forget he had the power to shock her with the stupid collar she wore.

If he did so in front of the girls, she'd never forgive him. She stopped on the landing of the outdoor stairs, gulping air.

Gav'n followed her out, slamming the door. At the same time, Jakk stalked up the stairs, also home early from work.

She fell apart. Angry, humiliated tears lost the fight to stay inside her and coursed down her cheeks. She turned her back on both of them and hugged her ribs.

Jakk stopped mid stride. Gav'n stepped closer but didn't touch her.

"I'm sorry I didn't believe you," she choked. "They really do hate me here."

"*Pashika...*" Gav'n's voice softened, laden with sympathy. "I wish to hell we'd been wrong."

"What did they do to you?" Jakk's voice was sharp, and he closed the distance between them, caging her against the railing, his front to her back.

She tried to choke back her tears, but only succeeded in making a horrible snuffling-snort. "Nothing," she quavered. "I'm sorry—I shouldn't have gone into the market. Gav'n told me to send Darley, but I wanted to see what they had. I was stupid."

The door opened a crack, and all three girls peeked out. In the yard beside theirs, the nosy neighbor woman craned her neck to look up at them.

"Come on," Gav'n urged, shooing the girls back in.

She had no intention of following them. She didn't want the girls to see her crying, nor did she want to face Gav'n and Jakk. She wanted to disappear. To go back to Earth. But, of course, that wasn't possible. A deep cold had set in, chilling her from the inside out.

Jakk's hands gripped her shoulders, his touch strong and sure. "Don't cry, little bird." His voice sounded strangled, as if the role of comforter was completely foreign to him. "Please come inside."

His touch warmed her, even though she didn't want it to.

"We won't let anyone hurt you again."

Something shifted. The pieces of her life fell apart and came together in a whole new configuration. She suddenly didn't know who she was, didn't know the man who stood behind her and seemed to care so much about her feelings. Was it possible she wasn't as alone as she'd imagined?

The twisting in her solar plexus eased. Her tears stopped, replaced by exhaustion. She let Jakk guide her into the house and up the stairs to their bedroom. Once there, he released her, shoving his hands into his pockets and pacing the room. Discomfort snaked between them.

She felt raw, her wound too fresh and open to defend herself. "Are you going to punish me?"

"No." He answered immediately, as if there was no consideration in his mind. He didn't comment on the lack of "Master" at the end of her question, either.

Wanting desperately to be alone, she headed for the bathroom. "I'm going to take a shower. I mean, may I, Master?"

"Yes. Okay. Take a shower. We'll talk later."

With a gulp of relief, she headed into the bathroom. She needed time to untangle her emotions. She'd expected a second assault from her "masters." Had they really chosen to stand by her, instead? Even when she hardly deserved it after disobeying again?

Because, in her book, that changed things. "Us against the world" was a lot different from "lonely alien against the entire planet."

But she needed to be careful. Just because they showed a little sympathy didn't mean they understood her, or respected her. And they definitely didn't trust her. So, no, they weren't anywhere close to being the family they purported to be.

Not yet. Maybe not ever.

~.~

JAKK WANTED to sentence every citizen in that store today to a public flogging. He wanted to round them up and make them all pay for diminishing their little alien. For taking the light and the life out of her. For making her cry.

Seeing her so demoralized *slayed* him. He knew Gav'n felt the same way. When he'd come downstairs, Gav'n had the girls rounded up, telling him exactly what had happened. Like any self-absorbed adolescent, Darley was angry and embarrassed about the whole thing, especially when she heard her uncles had intended for her to go in alone. Despite her young age, Pritzi had fully grasped the whole situation and recounted it with the same anger Jakk and Gav'n experienced on Mira's behalf.

They'd eaten in silence, Mira picking at the *madlyne* fruit she liked. She'd grown thinner since her arrival, and it worried him. She had found a few foods she could digest, sticking mostly to fresh fruits and vegetables.

Now, as she finished washing the dishes, he wanted to go to her, but he didn't know what to say. How did he make it better? *Don't worry, they'll grow to love you*, would be a lie. So would *Someday you'll feel at home here*. And the truth—*We know you're capable of so much more, but it turns us on to keep you as our sex slave*—probably wouldn't help things.

He closed the shutters against the dark.

Then opened them again, looking toward the bay. "Mira...girls? Who wants to go to the beach?"

"I do!" Pritzi cried, scrambling to her feet.

It was Mira's eyes he sought, and her startled gaze squeezed his heart. "When?" she asked.

"Now."

"Can we go now?" Doubt filled Darley's tone.

"Not legally," Gav'n said drily.

"Good thing we know the police commissioner."

Gav'n's lips quirked into a wry smile. "If my play-it-by-the-rules twin is up for breaking the law, I'm all in."

Jan and Mira joined Pritzi in jumping to their feet. Though Darley's customary scowl stayed in place, she scooted toward the bedroom. "Do we need our swimsuits?"

"If you want to swim."

Gav'n gaped at him.

Jakk knew his consequences-be-damned attitude was completely out of character, but this was the only thing he could think of to give to Mira. And he *needed* to soothe her. He couldn't stand feeling so damn helpless while she floundered and failed to find comfort in the world, the home, he'd provided her.

"Do I have a swimsuit?" Mira asked.

To his immense relief, he saw life back in her expression. A flicker of hope or happiness in her eyes.

"You can wear one of Darley's." Gav'n shot the eye-rolling adolescent a sharp warning look.

"May I, Darley?" Mira asked, following the girls into their room.

Gav'n raised his brows once they were alone.

"It was your idea."

Gav'n chuckled. "Crashing the beach after dark wasn't exactly the way I pictured it, but that's okay. It brings back the memories of our youth." He winked.

Jakk grinned. Their first threesome had been on a beach after dark when they were thirty-two. The dark had prevented the girl Gav'n had picked for them from noticing Jakk's eyes. They'd taken her virginity, and she'd taken theirs. She'd liked them well enough to ask for a second round, but before it happened, she'd seen Jakk in the light and had disappeared faster than a shooting star.

Their nieces emerged with Mira, who was stuffing towels into a large bag.

She caught his gaze and smiled.

His heart tumbled in his chest. He would do anything on his planet to win that smile every day. If only he knew how to make her happy.

He held out his hand, and she clasped it. Gav'n took the bag from her and held her other hand, leading her out the door after the racing children.

"Are we really going to the beach?"

"Yes."

"Why?"

He shrugged. "You deserve a change of scenery. We know being cooped up here all day is hard for you." He wanted to say more. He wanted to say it all. Whatever it took to let her know how much they needed her. Whatever it took to ease her restlessness. But he didn't know what those words sounded like.

She peered at his face in the darkness, but he didn't know how to show anything there, either.

They had to take both shuttles to fit them all, a problem he swore to rectify with a larger vehicle as soon as possible. The girls and Mira spilled out of the shuttles and raced for the sandy shore, kicking off shoes and stripping off their cover-ups as they ran.

He smiled, content to watch until Gav'n bumped his shoulder. "Last one in rides home alone."

The two tore off down the beach. Gav'n was in better shape, but Jakk's legs were longer so they were evenly matched. Sand kicked up behind their heels, the sound of their low chuckles made softer by the slap of surf against sand, the tinkle of girlish laughter from the water's edge.

They barreled past the girls. Gav'n scooped Pritzi into his arms, carrying her, shrieking with delight, straight into the depth of the bay.

Jakk dove into the cool water, savoring the shock to his system. He tried not to think about the possibility the water was contaminated from Mira's ship's fuel cell or how dangerous it was to let the girls swim in the dark. Or what would happen if they were caught.

They needed this. All of them. And yes, they still needed to ask Mira what she'd been researching on his computer, but that could happen later, after they healed some of their wounds together.

9

M ira carried the little amplifier out of the shed into the sunlight to see what she was doing. She'd been pilfering parts here and there, assembling everything she needed to make a speaker for Jakk's little music device. When the girls had seen her taking apart the oven, they'd grown excited, thinking she could fix anything. They'd produced a box of broken electronics their mother had stored in a cupboard. Mira had been pulling parts from the devices, and when she'd placed the order for the damaged thermocouple in the oven, she'd also ordered a few items for the amp without the men being any the wiser.

She'd told only Jan about her secret project, not trusting Pritzi not to let it slip, or Darley not to ruin it out of spite. She couldn't wait to install it in the house as a surprise. But it wasn't working yet. She tucked her hair behind her ear, wishing she had a voltmeter to test the output on the power boards she'd removed from all the broken devices. Between the mess of them, she should be able to cobble together something that worked.

A rustle from the nearby bushes caused her to look up, and she dropped the screwdriver in her hand. A wizened Pra'kirian face peered through the hedge at her. The nosy neighbor. Her heart rate increased, and she opened her mouth to speak, but her communication pad buzzed with a call. For the first time, it didn't show the photo of Jakk or Gav'n. Instead, it said Endermere Academy. She connected and looked back toward the bushes. The woman had disappeared.

"Hello?"

Apparently that wasn't the correct way to answer a call on Pra'kir, because the woman on the other end leaned her face into the screen, peering at her. "I'm trying to reach Mira Loquist, nanny to Darley Dacker."

"That's me, yes."

The woman scrunched up her nose. "We need you down at the school. Darley's been suspended for the day for fighting. We couldn't reach either of her uncles."

Mira set the powerboard down. "I'll be right there."

Damn. Her heart ached for Darley. The poor kid was so unhappy, acting out in every way she knew how. Yeah, she was a royal pain in the ass, but she was just a kid. A heartbroken kid.

She tossed the equipment back into boxes and stored them in the shed. Her little project would have to wait until later. She climbed into the shuttle and set the destination for the school.

When she arrived, thankfully, the students were in their classes, so the gawking was limited to the few people in the halls and at the front desk. The receptionist sent her into the director's office, where Darley slumped in a chair with red eyes and nose, arms across her chest, sniffling.

The director was an elderly female with curly white hair and long nails, painted black to match her suit. "Have a seat." She pointed at the chair across from her. "Darley was caught fighting with a boy in the play yard at noon. We do not tolerate fighting in any form. Because there was also the issue of her deliberate attempts to miss school by producing a false rash, I am considering permanently expelling her."

Mira chewed the inside of her lip. Without knowing anything about Pra'kirian schools, she wasn't sure of the best way to handle this.

She drew a breath. "Director, what counseling or help has the school provided to aid Darley and her sisters in dealing more effectively with the grief over their mother's death?"

The director blinked.

"You do remember their mother was killed mere weeks ago?"

"Well, of course I do," she snapped.

"Have you lost a parent, Director?"

The woman flushed. "I've lost both my parents. Of course, it was not as a child, but—"

"And how long did you grieve for them?"

The director paled, eyes misting. She swallowed. "For years."

Mira nodded soberly. "Can you imagine how hard it would be as a child? To lose both parents and suddenly have new caregivers, including one of the aliens indirectly responsible for your mother's death?"

Darley snuffled, obviously trying to hold back a sob, but Mira didn't turn.

The director, however, gave Darley a long, searching look. The severe lines of her face softened. She touched the tips of her fingers together. "The academy does not provide psychological assistance, but I can connect you with an agency that might be able to help."

She picked up her communication pad and wrote something. A moment later, Mira's pad beeped.

"You are right, I had not fully considered Darley's situation when I suggested expulsion. The academy will issue a warning. Any further disturbances will result in expulsion." She gave Darley a sharp look. "Understood?"

Darley bobbed her head up and down.

"Thank you, Director." Mira stood and walked to the door, waiting for Darley to exit first. "I'll bring her back tomorrow?"

The director nodded.

Darley wiped her cheeks as they walked to the shuttle, snuffling intermittently. An awkward silence hung between them.

Fuck it. Before Darley got into the shuttle, Mira pulled her into a rough embrace.

Darley froze, not moving, possibly not even breathing.

Mira released her as suddenly as she'd hugged her and walked around to her side of the shuttle. They rode home with Darley leaning her head against the window, staring out, tears dripping down her cheeks.

Poor baby. Mira wished there was something she could do or say to ease her pain. She let her stay in her room all afternoon, and even left her alone while she went back to pick up the younger two. Jakk and Gav'n arrived late that evening, and she and the girls were already sitting at the table eating dinner.

Jakk joined them first, the lines of his face tight and stern. "What happened at the academy today? My secretary said they called, and she gave them your contact code."

Gav'n pulled up a chair and sat as well.

"Darley had a little problem today, but everything is fine. We worked it out."

Darley lifted her cheek where it had been resting in her palm as she stirred her food listlessly.

"What trouble, exactly?" Gav'n asked. Jakk and Gav'n's gazes were sharp and they both appeared ready to bring the hammer down, hard.

She didn't want that. She shrugged, keeping her demeanor completely casual. "Don't worry about it. I handled it. Isn't that my job?" She smiled sweetly and tacked on the forgotten, "Master?"

Darley's mouth opened in shock, and Mira shot her a warning glance.

Suspicion glinted in Jakk's gaze as he considered both of them. He glanced at Gav'n, who shrugged.

"Are you certain this isn't something we need to know?" The clear warning in his tone that had her swallowing, but she held her ground.

"I'm sure. Everything has been handled."

Jakk nodded slowly. "Okay. Thank you for taking care of whatev-er...issue arose."

Darley took a sudden interest in her food, shoveling it in her mouth.

Gav'n watched them both thoughtfully but didn't speak.

Maybe, though she knew she'd done little to earn their trust, they'd actually let this go.

~.~

"Mira, we need to talk." Gav'n tugged Mira's jumper over her head and groaned. The no underclothing rule made stripping her a quick and delicious activity. One that nearly made him forget what he wanted to say to her.

He would never grow tired of studying her responsive, willing little body. If only they could bring her mind around to the same place.

Mira must have caught the flare of lust in his expression, because the corners of her mouth turned up and she sank to her knees to work the fastener on his pants.

He caught her arms and pulled her back up. "No, you can't talk with my dick stuffed in your mouth, as enticing as that scenario may be."

Jakk produced several silk ties from the closet, and Gav'n backed her up to the bed and tossed her into the center of it. The two brothers worked quickly to secure her wrists and ankles to the bedposts, spread wide.

He pulled out an implement he'd made for her. It was more for pleasure than pain, although it would produce a light surface burn. It consisted of a dozen lengths of soft rope, bundled at one end with a loop for a handle.

She writhed against the bonds, her green-blue eyes wary as he approached.

He climbed up on the bed and stood over her to trail the ends of the rope between her legs. She jerked and shivered. The scent of her arousal hit him like a powerful aphrodisiac. With a flick of his wrist, he brought the flogger sharply against her pussy.

She shrieked, eyes flying wide, the trembling extending down her legs now. Fortunately, the room was fairly soundproof.

"What have you been researching on Jakk's computer, love?" Another smack.

Jakk sat near her head and wound a length of thread around one of her nipples.

She struggled against her bonds, but he knew it was more out of fear than real pain. The vulnerability of her position and the part of her anatomy he'd chosen to punish, along with the mystery of Jakk's attentions, gave her no choice but to recognize their dominance over her.

"Did you think we wouldn't notice?" Jakk asked, tugging on the end of the thread and drawing her pinched nipple up toward the ceiling.

She cried out, panic flickering over her face.

"Did you find what you were looking for?" He delivered a harder smack to her pussy.

She shook her head rapidly. "No. No, Master."

He softened immediately, dropping to his knees between her thighs, soothing the burn away with his thumb over her slit. "If you want to know something, why don't you ask us?"

Her expression shuttered, and it hit him harder than he would've thought possible. She didn't trust them. She may trust them with her body, but she kept secrets, maybe still had plans to escape.

Jakk moved to her other side and wound a thread around the free nipple, imprisoning it, too, in his simple torture device. "Do you want to see your file?" he asked gently.

She stilled, a latent tension running through her body. Moistening her lips, she nodded. "Does it have...information on my shipmates?"

"Ah," he said, rewarding her communication with a generous

thrust of his thumb inside her channel, working her clit with his palm at the same time. "You're trying to find them. Is that it?"

She lifted her head as far as she could with her arms tied back. Her eyes were wide and desperate, and she hadn't breathed.

"*Pashika*," he said with soft regret. "We've talked about this already. You're not allowed to see them."

"*Please.*" Her head fell back on the bed, eyes tear bright. "They're my friends. I need to know they're okay."

Jakk shook his head. "Their placements weren't made public."

"You would know, though. Or could find out. You're a judge."

Jakk hesitated. "You're right. I probably could find out." He sighed. "Binnix, my Chief of Civil Police, took one of them, but I don't know which. And the general magistrate, himself, took the one who was badly injured."

"Brinley?"

"I don't know." Jakk tugged the thread of the second nipple, and she winced. He cupped and kneaded both breasts. "I am willing to make inquiries in the future. I'm willing to try to arrange a meeting, or get-together. But not yet. If I tried now, the request would be denied, perhaps forever. Give it a year or two, until each of you is settled in and your masters can vouch for your assimilation to Pra'kir."

She rolled her eyes and blinked back tears. "A *year* or two? How would you feel if I separated you from Gav'n for a year or two?"

He pursed his lips. "I would hate it, but if you did it to save my life, I would understand."

"Save my life?"

"The Council wanted you dead. This solution of fostering you out was presented by the general magistrate as a means of saving your lives. So we must stay within the guidelines they gave us—guidelines assuring the public is also safe from any perceived danger from you. Mira, we're asking you to trust us. Just like we gave you our trust to handle the problem with Darley on your own." Jakk stroked her cheek.

She sank into the bed a bit at that.

"We want your happiness. Can you believe that?" Gav'n slowly moved his thumb in and out of her again. Jakk leaned over and claimed her mouth, brushing his lips lightly across hers then licking into them.

She let out a soft moan and submitted, letting them pleasure her with their mouths, tongues, and hands until she came with a hoarse scream.

10

M ira stared at the amplifier pieces without seeing them. It was almost functional—a fuse had blown out, but it had worked for a moment. She couldn't focus on it, today, though.

That morning, after returning from dropping the girls at the academy, she'd researched the home address for the general magistrate. Unbelievably, Jakk had it programmed right into her communication device, which used to be his.

All she had to do was remove her collar and get in the shuttle and she could visit Brinley. The general magistrate was probably at work. Maybe she'd be home alone, like Mira. The idea of seeing another human—a friend—had her buzzing like an addict about to get a fix. So, yes, that meant she couldn't stop thinking about it, her mind looping on a single track.

She packed the amplifier parts and found the pair of bolt cutters she'd set aside after her first exploration of the shed. With the jaws open, she worked the lower blade under the collar at her neck.

The blade was too thick, though. *Ouch.* The tip of it cut the underside of her chin. Her throat spasmed, and suddenly the collar felt too tight, as if strangling her breath. She had to get the fucker off, now. With a snap of the jaws, she dug into the fragile skin at her throat again, slicing it open, but the collar also fell off.

Relief coursed through her. Chucking the bolt cutters, she jogged upstairs to the house to grab a washcloth for her cuts then back down to the shuttle. She had three-and-a-half hours before she needed to pick up the girls. She didn't know how far away the general magistrate lived, but hopefully it would be enough time.

She climbed into the bullet shuttle and programmed the general magistrate's address into the dash, which took a considerable amount of time, since she had to hunt and peck the characters she didn't recognize. Eventually, it seemed to work.

She drew a deep breath, fighting back the guilt.

No, she needed this. She didn't deserve to be held prisoner in Jakk and Gav'n's home. And if she played her cards right, they'd never know. Yes, she'd have to explain the severed collar. She would just say she felt like she was going to choke, which was true, and it had to come off. They'd punish her, but it wouldn't be the end of the world. Not like if they found out she'd gone to visit Brinley.

That would be bad.

She jumped the tracks onto the speedway and let the controls take over. Scenery flashed by as the shuttle drove toward the coast.

After about a half hour, she merged onto a speedway out of Endermere. She gasped once more at the incredible view she'd seen on her drive from prison. Turquoise water sparkled below. The shuttle zoomed along a set of coastal tracks hugging the edge of the cliffs.

But instead of feeling exhilarated as she sped along, her anxiety grew. A sense of dread expanded until it filled her, welling up to her throat. She ought to feel free. Joyful. Ecstatic to be her own master for a change, on her way to see a friend and fellow human. Why, then, did a foreboding sense of dread fill her gut? She'd felt more free that night at the beach, with her keepers.

Her masters.

Her lovers.

Shit.

Gav'n and Jakk would be furious and disappointed if they knew what she was doing. Coming here today was a violation of the trust they'd shown in sharing Brinley's location with her. The trust they'd given her to act as a parent to Darley.

Yes, that trust was still unsteady. But they'd asked her to believe in them. They'd promised to have her happiness and well-being at heart —to try to arrange a visit when timing was better. Did she believe they knew best? They certainly had about the grocery store visit. How had going rogue gone for her that time?

Fuck.

She didn't want them to lose faith in her. She tapped her fingers on the steering wheel, trying to make up her mind. Judging by the map program on the screen, she was almost there. But a lot of things could go wrong when she arrived. The general magistrate might be home. Or he might have some kind of staff or guards. And despite the fact she'd been thinking about finding her friends since the moment she left prison, it felt all *wrong.*

Clicking off the auto-programming, she spun into a turnabout track and punched up the program for home.

~.~

GAV'N WATCHED the tracker belonging to the family shuttle move along a map on his communication pad along the coast out of Endermere.

Meanwhile, the tracker in Mira's collar sat perfectly still at their home.

So, she had either removed the collar and was making a run for it, or their shuttle had been stolen.

Damn.

He was in the middle of an important police call—someone had broken in and stolen all the account cards from a bank during the night. Jakk was in court and couldn't be reached. He didn't want to send one of his men to investigate Mira and risk the Council finding out he and Jakk couldn't control her.

He shoved the communicator back into his pocket. He'd have to find her as soon as he could get away from this crime scene. He prayed she stayed with the shuttle or he'd have no way of finding her.

Where could she be going? Running away? Or was this just another one of her impulsive excursions, like flower picking or the grocery store visit? He sure as hell hoped it was the latter, but something in the way she'd wept and argued the night before made him think—

Yes.

That was it. She'd gone in search of her friend—what was her name? Brinley? He'd been to a party at the general magistrate's once. It was down the speedway she'd taken.

His relief at realizing her destination was short-lived, though. If the general magistrate caught her there, they stood a very good chance of having her taken away from them.

Damn.

He yanked his pad out again to study the tracker. Spinning it, he checked and rechecked her direction. She'd turned around since the last time he looked. What did that mean? Had she planned a secret meet-up with her friend? Had they passed some kind of information or materials? The detective in him dragged out every suspicion under their sun, each one making the stone in the pit of his gut grow heavier.

He shoved away the thoughts and marched through the crime scene, barking orders. The sooner they wrapped up their clue-gathering and packed to leave, the sooner he could find Mira and figure out what in the hell was going on.

An hour later, his police scanner buzzed with an incoming call from headquarters. "Commissioner, officers are responding to a call related to one of aliens. Neighbors report she has a bomb or some kind of weapon and is unsupervised and highly dangerous."

His ears buzzed. "What location?" he practically shouted, causing all his officers to stare.

"Three twenty-one Old Town Rd. Officers are responding, sir."

His world swooped and tilted. He raced toward the shuttle. The shouts and questions from his officers came as through a haze, sounding far away. He ignored them all, somehow making his hands work to open the door.

How had he missed this? His worst suspicions were playing out in the most public way. His career would never recover. Nor would Jakk's.

Jakk.

Mira's betrayal would kill him, his dream of having a female forever dashed.

Even Gav'n had been blinded by his desire for the little human. He'd somehow failed to see her duplicity, despite the fact she'd given plenty of warnings. The picked lock on her collar. The searched computer files. The need to connect with her shipmates.

Oh hell. What was Mira up to? He hated being blindsided like this.

His communicator buzzed again.

The academy. Aw, hell—nobody had picked up the girls. He let it go unanswered. They'd have to call Jakk this time.

He pushed the police shuttle to its maximum speed, screaming along the tracks, swerving to pass shuttles in his way. When he arrived at his sister's townhouse, twenty other police shuttles had surrounded the place, and news organizations crowded everywhere.

In the thick of it, Linat, their elderly neighbor, gesticulated, speaking rapidly to Binnix, his Chief of Civil Police. Mira lay face down on the ground, her wrists bound with plastic restraints used for juveniles, her legs spread. Her bare ass and pussy showed beneath the short dress they made her wear, and he cursed inwardly at his own idiocy in prohibiting underclothing.

He'd been so stupid. Toying with her like some kind of sexual plaything, when, in fact, she was a dangerous terrorist. Like his brother, he'd been thinking with his dick instead of his head.

But, as angry as he was—with himself and her—the sight of her being held that way enraged him. He didn't want everyone staring at her. And if anyone had hurt her, Gav'n would bash their teeth straight through their skulls.

He climbed out and slammed his shuttle door.

"Commissioner Ereen," one of the men sang out, announcing his presence, as was customary.

The crowd parted to let him stalk through. "Where's the weapon?" he demanded. "Show me." He purposely avoided addressing Mira. He couldn't even look at her, though he sensed her jerk of recognition when he'd spoken.

"It's right there, Commissioner," Chief Binnix said, pointing to a box of what appeared to be old electronics. He recognized it from his sister's cupboard. "What is it? What does it do?"

"We don't know, sir. The neighbor called in the emergency, sir." He pointed at the elderly neighbor still giving her report.

He picked up the wired device and examined it. "It's not a bomb. I don't believe it's a weapon of any kind, but we'll bring it in for a full examination." He spoke in a clear, authoritative voice, fully aware the news cameras recorded every bit of the drama. He wanted to give the message he saw no real danger but was taking the matter seriously and would thoroughly investigate to ensure public safety.

"We found these, too, Commissioner." One of the men showed him the bolt cutters and Mira's severed collar.

He steeled himself against the fresh wave of pain that cut him. "Get her up and into a shuttle." His voice came out cold and detached, though, inside, a torrent of emotions threatened to topple him. "We'll sort this out at headquarters."

Two men dragged her roughly to her feet, and it took every bit of willpower not to lunge forward and take custody of her himself. Not to yank their hands off her, smash their teeth in, and make certain no one ever touched her again.

But she wasn't his. She'd proven that. He and Jakk had fooled themselves into thinking they could tame her, keep her as their own. She'd never be theirs.

"Gav'n—?"

The wobble in her voice gutted him. He couldn't talk to her now, though. Not in front of all his men. Maybe not ever. He ignored her plea, didn't meet her gaze when she sought his eyes, tripping as they dragged her to the shuttle.

"Gav'n."

"Get her out of here," he growled, afraid he would come apart right there, ripped at the seams by his feelings for—yes, his *love* for—this human and the agony of losing everything. Her, his career, his brother's happiness.

She twisted, wrenching her shoulders against his men's hold on her, and the fear and pain on her face slammed through him like a stun gun.

He stumbled back, breath knocked out of him.

Mira...

But, no. He hardened himself against all the places she'd made him soft for her. He needed to be strong now.

For Jakk.

~.~

JAKK SHOVED his way into the police headquarters, the three girls in tow. He knew he should have brought them home, should have given them the illusion nothing had gone wrong, but he couldn't do it.

His life—their life—was in total crisis. The general magistrate would be here any minute, and he didn't even know what had happened yet. All he could gather from Gav'n was it was bad. Very bad.

"Uncle Jakk, why are we at police headquarters?" Pritzi asked. "Where's Mira?"

"She's here. Something happened—I don't know what."

Pritzi started crying softly, and he scooped her up into his arms. Her eyes widened in surprise. Had he never held her before? If he had, it hadn't been for comfort. Maybe to move her from one location to another. Like out of the shuttle. He suddenly realized how much he'd held back in his life. He'd never given affection freely, always ready for rejection, he supposed. Strange how Mira's easy acceptance of his care, his touch, had changed him.

He strode through headquarters and into Gav'n's office. His brother had some kind of electronic device and other parts and equipment strewn across his desk. Several policemen and a civilian, maybe an engineer, were examining the items.

"What happened?" he demanded.

"Find him an office," Gav'n barked at his men, indicating the engineer. To the civilian, he said, "I want to know exactly what that thing is and what it can do."

"Yes, Commissioner." The men exited and shut the door on their way out.

"Mira cut off her collar and drove somewhere up the coast. Probably to meet her shipmate. Then she came back and was working on building something. The neighbor called the police, saying it was a bomb."

He set Pritzi down, not wanting to squeeze her too tight as the tension in his body ratcheted higher. "What is it?"

"I don't know. Not a bomb. Maybe a communication device? Could they be trying to transmit back to Earth?"

His heart thudded hard against his chest. "Where is she? What has she said?"

His brother's jaw clenched. "I haven't been alone with her—it's been damage control from the moment I got the call."

"Take us to her."

"Why is Mira in jail, Uncle Gav'n?" Pritzi asked, her lower lip trembling again.

Gav'n picked up her hand. "We have some things to figure out, Pritzi. Mira may not be able to come back with us."

He'd known it was true, but hearing Gav'n say it out loud, like he'd already *accepted* it, turned his limbs to ice. They followed Gav'n through the halls to the holding cells, where Mira paced, wearing one of the yellow juvenile prison jumpers she'd had on when they first met. Two gashes marred her lovely throat where the tracking collar used to be.

"Mira," he croaked. "What in the hell is going on?"

Pritzi ran to the bars and stuck her little hand through, trying to reach Mira.

Mira whirled, eyes blazing. "Why don't you ask your brother?" she spat. She didn't take Pritzi's hand, but heartbreak crumpled her mouth when she faced the child.

"Mira, what's happening?" Darley asked.

Mira's jaw thrust out in a stubborn angle, and she crossed her arms over her chest. She glared furiously at Gav'n.

"Uncle Gav'n?" Darley prompted.

"Mira will probably be tried for treason."

The words shot across the prison and punched him in the face. He was surprised there wasn't blood dripping from his nose. *Treason?*

"We haven't determined yet what she was up to, but all of Endermere expects me to ensure their safety, and it's my job to keep Mira locked up until we understand what's going on."

"But what *is* going on?" Darley's voice rose in pitch.

"She was building some kind of electronic device in the shed. We believe she may be trying to communicate with her planet. In addition, she cut off her tracking device and went on unauthorized travel, possibly to visit one of her shipmates. We're investigating everything now." Gav'n sounded like he was reporting to the magistrate, rather than the family members who lived with and had grown to love Mira.

Mira covered her mouth, turning pale. Tears spilled down her cheeks and over her hand. She turned away from them, offering her back.

"What was the device, Mira?" Jakk asked.

She turned her back on them, shoulders hunched up to her ears.

"Get them out of here," Gav'n said.

He couldn't move. Nothing about this situation was right, yet he couldn't see any way out of it.

"Let's go," Gav'n said sharply, herding the children in front of him, out of the holding prison. "You shouldn't have brought them here."

Somewhere inside of Jakk, rage at his brother sparked and turned over, but icy cold devastation kept it from erupting. He felt numb, deadened.

Jan resisted Gav'n's shepherding, pulling away to run back. Gav'n picked her up by the waist, and she screamed, "No!"

Mira whirled, her expression registering the same shock they all felt to hear Jan speak. She rushed to the bars, but Gav'n was carrying Jan away.

Jakk stood frozen, staring at his female behind bars, lost.

"*Jakk,*" Gav'n hissed.

He shook himself, turned, and followed his family out, away from the woman he loved.

Away from his ruptured heart.

Away from any chance he'd ever had at happiness.

~.~

THE ONLY THINGS keeping Mira from falling to her knees were her sweaty palms hanging onto the prison bars. Had she really just lost her new family? And over what? A fucking shuttle ride that hadn't even ended with a visit to Brinley.

Where was that trust they were supposed to be showing each other?

Hell, she supposed she'd violated it one too many times. And the highly public nature of her capture put both her men—God, were they still hers?—in a bad position.

Gav'n hadn't even looked at her during the arrest. He'd abandoned her completely, already written her off. Did he really believe she'd been trying to communicate with Earth with that primitive technology? The idea was ludicrous.

And while rationally she understood if he accepted that explanation, he must feel completely betrayed by her right now, nothing softened the bite of his complete lack of caring.

She slid to her knees on the floor, blessed numbness setting it. She'd fucked everything up. She shouldn't have driven out to see Brinley, should've waited and trusted her men, her masters, to arrange something.

Her mind ran over the time she'd spent with Jakk and Gav'n and the girls, remembering every day. In hindsight, she wished she'd done a million things differently. Why had she resisted Jakk and Gav'n and the place they tried to provide for her? Now that she stood to lose it, to lose everything—probably even her life—she wished she'd appreciated what she'd had. Two men who paid more attention to her and her pleasure than anyone had in her life. Three children who needed her. Friendship. Family. Love. Steaming hot sex. What wasn't to love about all that?

If she had it to do over, she never would've chipped away at their trust by picking the lock on the collar that first week, or disobeying orders by going into the store or gathering flowers. She would've had more faith in Jakk and Gav'n from the start and opened up about her difficulties and desires.

Now it was all too late. They thought she was a terrorist. The citizens of Endermere hated and feared her. Without Jakk and Gav'n to defend her, she was done. She just wished the girls hadn't had to see her like this, didn't have to lose another person in their lives. It wasn't fair to them.

~.~

Gav'n carried his kicking niece out into the hall. Jan cried, her little face pale and drawn.

"Get them home," he barked at Jakk, furious with his brother for bringing them there in the first place. They shouldn't have seen Mira like that.

Jan and Pritzi clung to each other, weeping. Darley appeared lost, her customary scowl gone, brows drawn up together.

Jakk wasn't any better. He'd vacated his body, which stood as an absent shell.

He tugged them all down the hall, toward the front door, just in time to meet the general magistrate.

"What in the hell is going on?" Rowth growled.

"General Magistrate, we're getting to the bottom of things right now." He attempted to exude confidence and capability. Like he wasn't about to lose his job and Mira in one fell swoop.

"Uncle Gav'n." Jan tugged on his sleeve.

"What happened, exactly?" Rowth barked.

He opened his mouth, preparing to launch into a rehearsed explanation.

"Uncle Gav'n."

He froze, realizing why the rest of his family had gone dead silent. Jan was talking again--beyond the single utterance she'd yelled back in the jail. *Jan.*

Her tear-streaked face tipped up to him, desperation apparent in the crinkle of her brow. "I know what Mira was building in the shed."

The air left his lungs in a whoosh. "One moment, Your Honor," he said to the general magistrate, lowering to one knee in front of his niece. "What was Mira building, sweetheart?"

"Something to make Uncle Jakk's music louder. She called it an...amfliyer, I think."

His body turned to stone. "Amplifier?"

"Yes. We gave her the parts Mama had put in the cupboard—the broken stuff. She liked to take things apart to see how they worked. Like the way she fixed the oven. She was working on a surprise for

Uncle Jakk. She told me not to tell until it was ready. She needed a new part."

Relief coursed through him. Relief and dread at what he'd done to Mira—was it too late to fix things? He straightened up and faced the general magistrate. "Your Honor, it seems my niece has solved the mystery. Our elderly neighbor called the police today when she saw Mira tinkering with old electronics. Apparently, she thought Mira was building a bomb. We had to be sure, of course. Better safe than sorry. So we brought the equipment and the human in here until we'd sorted things out. I will have our expert engineer verify what my niece has shared, but it sounds like we have a satisfactory explanation." He attempted what he hoped was an affable smile.

The general magistrate narrowed his eyes. "Why didn't she tell you that herself? Surely you questioned her. What did she tell you she's been building?"

His stomach twisted. "I hadn't had a chance to question her yet, Your Honor."

Rowth gave him a cold stare. "I see."

"The press were there when I arrived, so it's been damage control until now."

"Get the child's word verified immediately so the public can be calmed. The last thing we need is more hysteria around the aliens."

"Yes, Your Honor. Right away, sir."

The focus had finally returned to Jakk's eyes. "I'll get the children out of here, then. We'll be waiting for you to bring Mira home before bedtime." He caught the blame in his brother's tone. Not that he wasn't already wallowing in a whole pile of it.

He had made a terrible mistake. At least, he hoped. There was still the matter of where Mira had gone, and he would question her about it. Which is what he should've done in the first place.

He bowed to the general magistrate and headed to the office where the expert engineer examined the equipment. When he verified Jan's story, exclaiming over her ingenuity, and even installing the missing part—a fuse—to make the thing work, it took all he could do not to run to Mira's prison cell.

Oh hell.

Mira's blonde head was bowed and leaning against the bars where she knelt.

"Open her cell," he barked, stepping through the door the moment the guard opened it. "Lock us in." The door clanged shut behind him. "Mira," he said softly, lifting her to her feet.

She came back to life, then, shoving him away.

"You were making a surprise for Jakk. For his music? Jan told us."

That got her attention.

"Yeah, she's speaking full sentences. For you, *pashika*."

Mira's lips trembled, eyes swimming with tears.

"I'm sorry I didn't let you tell me sooner."

She abruptly turned away and, when he touched her, retreated into the corner of the cell, her back firmly to him.

"Okay, I know you're mad." He followed her there, tried to turn her around, but she resisted. He covered her eyes with his hand and spun her to face him. "You don't want to look at me? You don't have to, baby. But I need to see you."

She submitted to his touch, facing him, but her mouth formed an angry pout.

"Forgive me, baby," he said softly, not wanting the guards to hear their private conversation. "I didn't know what to think. Tell me where you drove today." He inched his hand away from her eyes, and she blinked up at him.

Her face screwed up. "I wanted to visit Brinley. I drove most of the way there, but I changed my mind and came home. Please believe me —I never saw her. I'm sorry, Gav'n."

Her story aligned with what he'd seen on the tracking device. He wrapped his arms around her and pulled her little body against his.

"It's all right, *pashika*. I'm going to get you home now. Where you belong. We'll work everything out, I promise."

She pressed her face against his chest, dampening his shirt with her tears.

"Come on, baby. Jakk and the girls are waiting up for you. Let's get you out of here."

The guard responded to his call and opened the gate. She changed back into her clothing, and he picked up the now-functioning amplifier. He had to resist the urge to carry her out of there. He wanted to feel her close, to know she was really still his—theirs. Because one thing he knew for certain—he would never let her go again.

11

Part of Mira wanted to stay mad at Gav'n for the way he'd abandoned her. Her heart still ached from the fresh wound, but the way he kept looking over at her as he raced home, as if he was afraid she might disappear at any moment, did a lot to ease the pain.

When they parked at home and got out, Gav'n scooped her up into his arms and headed toward the stairs. Only to be blocked by the bitch of a neighbor who had reported her. The old woman eyed Mira with ill-concealed curiosity. Her Mekron family member crouched behind her.

"Linat," he spat. He set Mira down but tucked her against his side. "If you have a concern about the activities of any of my family members, I'd prefer you to talk to me personally, rather than upset the entire city without cause." He pinned her with a meaningful glare.

She flushed, backing up a step and almost tripping over the Mekron, Arnc.

"This is Mira. She's a very talented engineer who was sweet enough to invent a device to amplify Jakk's music player. She's a member of our family. We've fostered her, as you fostered Arnc."

Mira forced a weak smile.

"Now, if you'll excuse us, your emergency call to the police—*the organization, I might remind you, I run*—disrupted our entire day and upset the children. We'd like to get home so Mira can put them to bed at a decent hour."

"Oh, yes, of course." Linat shuffled out of their way, flushing.

Gav'n picked Mira up again, this time with her legs straddling his waist. He carried her up the stairs, but, instead of opening the door, he pushed her back against it and nipped at her neck. His cock pressed against the notch between her legs, hot and hard. When his lips brushed one of the cuts under her throat, he reared back, brows slamming down as his thumb touched the wound lightly.

"No more collars." His warm brown eyes found hers, solemn with promise. "Either we trust you or we don't. And we do."

Her remaining anger at him ebbed away, and she went soft against the door, her body pliant and willing. "I promise to be worthy of your trust."

He buried his face in her hair, kissing the place where neck met shoulder. "No more leaving without permission." He lifted his head. His hand lightly caged her throat, and his gaze turned intense, challenging.

She tensed but then nodded. "Yes, Master."

"You'll be punished for today." The growly way he spoke told her it would be the kind ending with all their satisfaction.

She wended her fingers through his hair, pulling his mouth down to hers. "Yes, Master," she murmured and kissed him.

He immediately took control, claiming her mouth with a hard, demanding kiss that reminded her who owned her, who she'd always belong to.

She groaned when he pulled away.

"We'd better go in," Gav'n said.

She tried to ignore the heat and pulse between her legs as he pushed the door open and carried her inside.

Jakk and the girls were waiting, and they all rushed over,

surrounding them. Gav'n refused to put her down, so she was encased in a giant octopus hug.

"Are you mating Mira, Uncle Gav'n?" Pritzi demanded when he kissed Mira full on the lips again.

She twisted in his grasp, seeking Jakk's eyes. She didn't feel she belonged more to one brother than the other.

"Mira's going to be both Jakk's and my mate," Gav'n said. "Right, baby?"

Her heart skipped a beat as her chest swelled. "Yes, okay."

Gav'n looked at Jakk. "Okay with you, brother?"

Jakk leaned his head toward both of theirs, and the three touched foreheads. "Yeah. It's perfect."

"Well, put me down so I can get the girls to bed."

Gav'n gave her ass a squeeze and eased her feet to the floor. "We love you, little human. I love you."

"And I love you," Jakk said.

"I love you, too," Pritzi trilled.

She squeezed Pritzi, stroking her soft brown hair. "I love you so much, peanut."

"What's a peanut?"

"Someone who's small, like you."

She turned and enveloped Jan in an embrace. "Jan, thank you for speaking up for me. I needed you today, and you came to my rescue. That's what family members do. I love you."

Jan's ears turned pink, but she smiled.

Darley stood slightly farther away, as if a hug would be the worst thing that could happen to her, but Mira caught her up in one, anyway. "Darley, I can't wait to get to know you better. I'm so glad we're friends."

Relief and surprise mingled on Darley's face, and she threw her arms around Mira for a second quick hug before ducking her head and heading for the bedroom.

"All right, girls. It's bedtime. Let's go."

She tossed a smile over her shoulder at the two giant men

watching her with goofy looks on their faces. "See you in a little bit."
She winked.

~.~

JAKK HAD the strap out for Mira's punishment. Neither he nor Gav'n
was inclined to give her a long, drawn-out session.

"Is it really okay with you? That we share her?" Gav'n asked.

He turned, surprised. "Wasn't that always the plan?"

"I know, but..." Gav'n hesitated. "I could find a mate of my own. I
should. But I don't want to."

Jakk shook his head. "I don't want you to, either. She cares for us
both." He believed that now. She'd been working on a present for
him. For *him*, the man no female would ever have. He'd never
believed he'd have a female who worked for or cared about his affection and wasn't just there because of Gav'n. So, yeah, maybe he
should snatch this one up for himself, but that wouldn't be fair to
Gav'n. "We share her," he said firmly. "We never make her choose.
With the amount of time we spend working, she'll need both of us."

Gav'n dropped a hand on his shoulder. "Are you sure?"

"Yes. Just don't arrest her again."

Gav'n ran his fingers through his hair. "I messed up today. It's my
job. I suspect the worst in people because that's often what I see."

"She forgives you."

"I'll make it up to her."

Mira pushed open the door, her eyes soft, even when she took in
the strap in his hand. "Clothes off, Mirella-mine," Gav'n murmured,
walking to her and unbuttoning her jumper before she could. He slid
it down over her shoulders and then her hips, revealing her lush,
naked body underneath.

So beautiful. So incredibly perfect for them. To think they might
have lost her today.

Gav'n led her to the bed and sat on the edge, holding her hands. "Bend over and put your head on my lap, little one. Jakk's going to whip you for taking off your collar and leaving without permission. But we also recognize you turned around and came home, and we thank you for that."

"I'm sorry—for everything. I know I've been as difficult as the girls—rebelling at every turn. Thank you for not giving up on me." Folding at the waist, she presented her delectable bottom.

He smelled the scent of her arousal and closed his eyes a moment to savor it. "Beautiful girl," he murmured, changing the strap to his other hand to stroke her ass with his palm.

Gav'n had his fingers tangled in her hair, his other hand stroking up and down her side.

He cleared his throat, forcing himself to complete their duty to punish her. "We'll make it ten," he said, gripping the strap and drawing it back. "You don't have to count, but if you stay in position, I'll make it fast."

He didn't go easy on her, bringing the strap down with punitive force, allowing minimal time between strokes.

Mira shrieked and danced. Gav'n helped her stay in place, stroking and calming her. When it was over, her twitching ass wore ten red stripes, and she hugged Gav'n's waist, trembling.

Before he could help her stand, she fumbled at Gav'n's pants.

Oh hell, yeah.

He stroked her welted ass, bringing his fingers between her legs to delve into her ample nectar.

She moaned and spread her legs wider as she gripped Gav'n's cock.

"You want both your masters' cocks, *pashika*?" He pulled out his own and rubbed the head along her slickened slit.

"Yes, Master." Her breathy voice had him shoving into her much sooner than he'd planned.

She gasped, her tight channel squeezing him.

He gripped her hips to hold her steady as he drove slowly, deliberately, in and out while she licked around the head of Gav'n's cock.

"Who do you belong to, little one?"

"You," she panted. "Both of you."

He grinned, shoving in with more force, careful to keep her hips still so she didn't choke on Gav'n's cock. "That's right, little one. You want both our cocks at once, tonight, don't you?"

"Mmm hmm," she hummed, sucking on Gav'n's cock like a good girl.

He caught Gav'n's eye and grinned, pulling out.

"I take bottom," his brother offered.

Mira's head jerked up as she suddenly understood what she'd agreed to. "Wait—what?"

They didn't give her any time to protest. Gav'n slid back on the bed, lifting under her armpits to pull her with him. "Ride me, baby." He lay on his back and arranged her hips over his.

Her head dropped back as she took him inside her.

Gav'n shuddered with pleasure. "Good girl," he choked, snapping his pelvis up while pulling her hips down.

Jakk grabbed the sex oil, ditched his pants, and crawled up behind her on his knees. As Jakk coated his cock in oil, Gav'n pulled her torso down over his, kissing her while continuing to thrust up into her.

Jakk dribbled oil down her crack, and she lifted her head, but Gav'n held her captive, kissing away her protests as he rocked in and out of her with a steady rhythm.

"This ass belongs to me tonight," Jakk rumbled, using his thumb to massage a generous amount of oil into the tight ring of muscle. Her anus squeezed and released in response. He brought the head of his cock to her back entrance, and Gav'n stopped thrusting, holding her still for him.

"Open for Jakk, baby," Gav'n murmured. "Relax."

He pushed slowly, easing in little by little, giving her time to adjust to the extreme stretch and invasion of double penetration. When he'd entered fully, she mewled, and both he and Gav'n held still.

"Okay," she whispered.

He gave a short pump. Gav'n did the same. The two alternated, working her ass and pussy in tandem.

From her throaty cries, he knew how intense it must be for their little human. "Please...please...please," she whispered. "Oh, please. Oh God."

He and Gav'n began to thrust at the same time, filling her simultaneously.

She tossed her blonde hair, her cries growing faster, shorter.

His own need overcame his control. Afraid he would hurt her if he let go, he buried his cock deep in her ass and pumped his hips over her, moving for all three of them, shoving her down over Gav'n's cock with each short thrust.

All of their voices joined in union, Gav'n's guttural grunts mingling with Mira's high-pitched keen and his own roar as all three came crashing to a glorious finish together. He came so hard, stars danced before his eyes.

He collapsed over them, their breaths mingling in a choir of pants and sighs.

"Ours," he murmured, stroking Mira's golden head.

"Mmm hmm," Gav'n mumbled with satisfaction.

"I love you guys," Mira mumbled.

He wrapped his fist in her hair to pull her head up, seeking her mouth with his. They kissed, lips tangling and sucking. "I love you, little human. You belong to us, and we're never letting you go. Understand?"

"I belong with you," she agreed.

EPILOGUE

Mira gazed up the hillside.

"How's this spot?" Jakk called from the top of a majestic plateau.

Pritzi raced up the flowered hillside to join him. She spun around with her arms out. "It's perfect! Come and see, Mira!" The little girl wore a lavender dress, a wreath of braided flowers in her hair.

She, Jan, and Darley wore matching wreaths and the same style dresses, but in their own favorite colors—Jan in turquoise and Darley in red. Mira's simple dress was white, as was the custom on Earth. She clutched a giant bouquet of wildflowers, picked by all five of them. Gav'n held her other hand, steadying her as she hiked up the mountainside toward the rest of the family.

They'd decided to have the wedding—or mating, as they called it —ceremony alone. No witnesses besides their family. It wasn't a true, legal ceremony—that would be impossible with Mira's status on Pra'kir, but it was a formal way to mark their union as a family. They'd considered inviting Jakk and Gav'n's parents, who had embraced Mira's sudden presence in their children and grandchildren's lives, but decided they wouldn't be able to make the hike.

The mountainside was similar to the one where she'd stopped to pick wildflowers with the girls, only it stood high enough they could see the ocean. She reached the summit where Jakk and the girls waited and turned around, breathing it all in.

Everything about it was perfect.

"Okay, so now what?" Gav'n asked. The entire family had participated in the evolving plan for the day. Pritzi had insisted on the flower wreaths. Darley had picked out their dresses. Jakk had chosen the location.

"I have something for you." She pulled a little silk bag from Gav'n's pocket. "On Earth, we have a tradition of giving rings for marriage, so I had a ring made for each of us. They all match, see?" She tipped the bag upside down, and six gold rings rolled into her palm. They were simple matching bands, inscribed on the inside with the words *Family Forever*.

The girls reached for them, but she closed her fingers and lifted her hand high.

"Wait, wait, wait. There's a ceremony that goes with the giving of rings. You see, on Earth, the ring is a symbol of love, which has neither beginning nor end. It goes on your fourth finger, which on humans is the warmest, and, therefore, the closest to the heart."

The girls jockeyed for position, lining up in a row before her, hands held out with the fourth finger aloft.

"With this ring, I thee wed." She slid the smallest ring onto Pritzi's finger. "Wear it as a symbol of my love." She repeated the vow with each child. When she moved on to face Jakk, a sudden shyness overcame her.

Jakk reached for her, tugging her up against his body. "Why are you nervous, little human?" he murmured. "You're ours, whether you give me that ring or not."

Gav'n stepped behind her, sandwiching her between them. "Where's your ring, *pashika*? We'll put it on you together."

Face warm, she opened her palm and picked out her ring. Gav'n slid it on her finger, and Jakk lifted it to his lips, kissing it. "With this ring, we claim you forever."

She giggled. "Those aren't the words."

Gav'n flashed his roguish smile. "I forget them." He held out his ring finger. "Give me mine."

She slid one of the huge rings on his finger. "With this ring, I thee wed. Take it as a symbol of my love." She repeated the words as she bestowed the last ring on Jakk's finger.

"What do we do now?" Jakk asked.

"We hold hands," Jan offered. She'd been talking more, though still not nearly as much as Pritzi.

"Like this?" Gav'n joined hands with her and Pritzi.

"No, in a circle," Jan said. "No beginning, nor end."

"Like love," Darley finished.

"Like love," Jakk murmured. "I love you all. You know that?"

The girls giggled, and her eyes misted. "I love you all, too."

"Me too."

"Me too."

"Me too."

"Me too."

"Now what do we do?" Gav'n asked.

"We eat cake," she declared.

"What's cake?" Pritzi demanded.

"It's the most wondrous food you've ever tasted. And I figured out how to make it on Pra'kir. But it's at home. Last one to the shuttles is a rotten egg!" She tossed her bouquet over her head and ran, pell-mell, down the steep hillside for the shuttles.

Whoops and shrieks sounded behind her as her family followed, the sounds of their joy echoing on the rocks and pinging back, straight into her heart.

READ ALL THE CAPTIVES
OF PRA'KIR BOOKS

CAPTIVES OF PRA'KIR, BOOK 1: BINDING BRINLEY

Captives of Pra'kir, Book 1
Binding Brinley
By
Maren Smith

Excerpt:

H e noticed her silence and it was enough to distract him from the news. "I sense you are unhappy."

"You think?" Brinley asked caustically. "What could I possibly have to be unhappy ab—oh, wait." She held up her bound wrists in emphasis. "Among many other reasons, this might have something to do with why."

"That is a temporary security measure and one that will eventually be discarded." He turned back to his news.

"When?"

"Just as soon as I can trust you. Five... perhaps ten years from now."

Five or ten *years*? Her temper spiked again. "Maybe if I knew I was going to be treated fairly in a place that isn't another prison, I'd be more willing to be trustworthy."

He stared at her for so long she began checking the open stretch of rail ahead of them.

"Do you want me to drive?" she offered.

"No."

"Then would you? One fiery crash per lifetime is enough for anybody." She settled back in her seat, fidgeting with the cuffs, twisting her wrists until it felt as if the rough plastic edges were cutting into them. "Watch the road."

"We aren't going to crash, fiery or otherwise," Rowth soothed again. "It's all perfectly automated, and I'm not taking you to another prison. I'm taking you to my home."

"Can I leave?" she demanded.

"No."

"Then it's a prison. Watch the road."

"I don't need to 'watch the road'," Rowth said, not quite rolling his eyes. "The shuttle can handle itself."

"If that were true, it wouldn't come with controls. If you can't trust your own car, what hope do I have?"

"Why do I feel you are trying to start an argument with me?"

"Oh, I don't know," Brinley said, too busy clutching the handle to notice the warning in his frown. "Maybe because you drugged me, you're holding me prisoner, and now you're trying to scare the shit out of—watch the damn road! Oh my God, slow down!" Was it her imagination or did she really just feel the car come off the rails on that last corner? "You're trying to kill me, you sadistic—"

"Watch your tone." Releasing the controls, Rowth sat back in his seat far enough to face her fully. "You are fine. You are safe. But you might not be if you speak to me like that again. Let me explain something you seem not to have realized. I am the only person responsible for your current and future wellbeing, and there are consequences associated with trying to upset me for no good reason."

"No good reason?" Letting go of the handle, Brinley shook her bound wrists at him. "Think about it carefully. *No* good reason?"

"Nobody upsets me," Rowth replied. "Think about *that* carefully. Nobody. Not one person on the whole of this planet."

She gave him a toothy, unamused smile. "Not anymore."

"Do you want me to take you to the cellar first thing when we get home?" He said it as if it were a threat. "Because if you do, I have an old barrel that you may well find yourself stretched over before the night is out."

Her smile vanished even as her eyebrows rose. "What, like stretched on a rack? What comes next, flogging? Waterboarding? Are you going to stick an anal pear up my ass and see how wide you can open it before I scream?"

His expression underwent the most subtle change, drifting from unreadable to damned unreadable, but with a touch of approval. "So, your people have a precedent."

"Only if you're Torquemada." When he only blinked at her, she grudgingly supplied, "He was a Grand Inquisitor several hundred years ago."

"Inquisitor?"

"A religious torturer during the Spanish Inquisition."

Shifting in his chair, Rowth put his hands back on the vehicle's control stick. "My translator is having difficulties with much of what you say, but I am not your Torquemada. However, magistrates do often make inquiries, so I suppose that does make me an inquisitor of a sort." He studied the rail ahead of them. "And I am rather grand." She stared at him, silent in her incredulity, until he added, "You'd do well to keep that in mind, too, before you go deliberately seeking ways to prick my temper."

"I don't know what I was thinking," she deadpanned.

He shrugged. "You're an alien, a female, and incredibly young. For a short time, at least, I am willing to be both patient and stern while you learn how best to mold yourself to our ways and become a productive member of society."

〜

Binding Brinley

The only member of the SS Reconnaissance not to reach the shuttle in time, Brinley Lawson never thought she'd survive the crash. Nobody expected her to survive the healing process either, but now, in the home of the same magistrate who tried and found her guilty of crimes against Pra'kir, Brinley knows only that she can't stay any more than she can leave. However, if he thinks she'll blindly obey any command he makes, then he can think again. His punishments might leave her body aching, both with pain and sensual arousal, but Brinley has never been a woman to blindly submit to anyone, much less an alien lawyer.

Everyone is guilty of something. That is the motto dominant Rowth Lashat lives by and he doesn't consider the diminutive human female lying battered and broken in her hospital bed to be any different. Not until she issues that first irresistible challenge and suddenly he finds his authority being pricked at every turn. Still, it's not her constant defiance that forces him to bend the rules, bringing her into his home, into his care... and even into his bed. It's something much more important. Though winning her submission calls to him, it's Brinley's cooperation that Rowth needs. Hopefully, before it's too late.

She survived the crash.
He'll make her wish she hadn't.
Captives of Pra'kir.

Now Available!

CAPTIVES OF PRA'KIR, BOOK 2: MATED AGAINST HER WILL

Captives of Pra'kir, Book 2

Mated Against Her Will

By

Dinah McLeod

Excerpt:

Her brow furrowed as she scowled at him. "Well, you know what, I *don't* want you to spank me, not for pleasure, or anything else. Maybe I did, but I don't anymore. You're arrogant to think that every woman must want you. You're arrogant, and you're a jackass."

He listened to her angry tirade until she stopped. She was still glaring at him, and breathing hard, her nostrils flaring. Still, he found her insatiably attractive. He never would have thought he would enjoy being yelled at—indeed, no woman on his planet had ever dared—and maybe it was simply because he was thinking of spanking her pale, gorgeous ass again, but somehow, her little speech just made his cock harder. He had to have her.

"Go get me a switch from that tree over there," he instructed as he pointed. He was careful not to let his voice betray his feelings of desire.

"Fine," she snapped. She whirled around and took three steps toward the tree before spinning to face him again. "You know what? No. I will not. I'm tired of you acting like I'm some...some animal you have to tame! I will not be treated like this, and I am *not* going to fetch an implement for you to beat me with! If you want it, get it yourself!"

Binnix stepped toward her, his long legged strides closing the distance between them almost before she could realize what was happening. Then he captured her face between his hands, lifted her effortlessly and kissed her.

When he set her back down again the look on her face was positively dazed.

"Get me the switch I asked you for, Sarai."

"I...what did you do to me?"

"I kissed you," he replied matter-of-factly.

"Was it...do you...was it magic?"

He chuckled softly. "It might have been for you."

"I...I feel so strange."

"I can see that. Get me the switch now—don't make me tell you again."

"Or what?" she asked. She didn't sound defiant this time—all of the anger had melted out of her voice. She seemed merely curious and Binnix was happy to satisfy her curiosity.

"Or I'll whip your bottom to ribbons, my darling."

She bit down on her bottom lip, looking at him with wide, limpid blue eyes before she nodded once.

He was pleased that she'd chosen to obey, and just as thrilled to watch her walk away. How had he not noticed just how voluptuous her backside was? Her hips were wide, creating quite the eye-catching sight when she was viewed from behind. She had such a tiny waist, which made her ass stand out all the more. It was a beautiful sight anytime, though his favorite was when it was bare and over his knee. He was going to branch out, however—no pun intended—and see what he thought of it bare and bent over while she hugged a tree and waited for the lash of the switch. Though he couldn't say for sure, he was nearly certain that he would find it just as pleasurable.

Mated Against Her Will

Sarai, a top communication specialist, is thrilled when offered a coveted spot aboard the SS Reconnaissance and a one-way trip to Earth's first terraforming project: Zeta 12. However, elation quickly turns to panic when their shuttle goes down, crash-landing on an unfamiliar planet. After a brief trial, which she is neither invited to witness nor participate in, she finds herself being handed over to an alien "foster parent."

This species might look human, but larger-than-life, superbly sculpted and with scolding glances that had a way of turning women into submissive puddles (or was that just her?), the Pra'kir are anything but. From the moment she is taken prisoner, the only thing Sarai can think of is escape. She is hard at work trying to accomplish just that when she stumbles onto something that changes how she thinks about her alien captor...and herself.

Despite his personal tragedy when the humans' shuttle crashed, Binnix must put his resentment aside to focus on the strange, yet alluring creature that is now his houseguest. Though he reluctantly accepts his task to mold her into a model citizen, he is soon surprised to find he has feelings for her. He tries to keep his growing emotions at bay, but soon the desire to tame her overtakes him and he must know what it feels like to dominate such a soft, yet stubborn woman.

A woman who longs for home can't possibly find it in herself to give up her dreams for the alien who demands her submission...can she?

Now Available!

CAPTIVES OF PRA'KIR, BOOK 4: THE ALIEN'S MARK

Captives of Pra'kir, Book 4

The Alien's Mark

By

Megan Michaels

Excerpt:

"You know what's expected."

"But—"

"No." Xan stopped setting up his tray, putting his hands on his hips, exasperated with his girl. "Do I need to tie you down?"

"No, Master. I'll be good." Her eyes darted around the room, looking toward his lab.

"I know where you want to go, but you'll have to behave first, or the privilege will be taken away. What would take away your visitation, girl?"

She pulled her lip between her small white teeth. "Moving my hands from above my head. Uhm...I need to keep my legs splayed open for your procedures and be very still."

"Yes." He nodded toward her solemnly, raising his eyebrows in warning. "Or you could cause injury, but more than that you'd be a sad girl for the rest of the day, waiting for visitation tomorrow."

Her heart dropped, she had to see the test tube—*needed* – to see it. The thought of waiting another day made tears threaten to fall. "I'll be good."

"I know you always believe you will be, but you have a way of dashing even your hopes in that regard...often. What else?" He methodically places his tools and swabs just the way he liked them, waiting for her answer.

"I need to have a respectful attitude, guarding my tone and words."

"You seem to know the words, but there's a disconnect with your actions. Isn't that so, bad girl." His dark eyebrows were knit above the eyes so dark that the pupils couldn't be seen. He'd been drilling the rules into her for months now—and her ass—and she knew how to repeat them in rote form.

"I don't think so." She blinked innocently up at him. Whenever possible she reinforced that she tried and that she was indeed a good girl. *Always convey your desire to be obedient to your captor.*

Turning his head, he addressed their nurse, "Ganza, I'd like to hear your opinion on the matter of Miss Blythe's attitude and respect regarding obedience to the rules."

The very large woman stepped forward, the fabric on her crisp black dress and white apron whispering as she walked, her hand sweeping over her hair caught up in a severe bun on the back of her head. "It's been my experience that Blythe is fiery and sassy, some days it seems beyond repair, but when she puts her mind to it, she is as sweet as a kitten, Sir."

"Indeed, and just as cuddly as one too, but your observation is sound. As always, Ganza. Thank you." He gave his faithful employee a slight bow before wagging his finger toward Blythe. "I suggest you still that sassy tongue, or I may have to put it to good use. I have ways of keeping an open mouth occupied."

Blythe's hips squirmed on the metal table, her arousal climbing.

Although she'd never admit it to him, sucking his cock – or even thinking about it – had become a great source of pleasure. The length and girth of a Pra'kirian cock was something to behold. Initially, it'd been more than she thought she'd ever adjust to, but over time, she loved nothing more than displaying her love for it.

"It doesn't appear to be a serious threat to her, Sir." Ganza tried—unsuccessfully—to hide a grin.

He shot a glare at the nurse, watching her quickly fix her face. "Oh, but it is. She likes to *think* she'll enjoy it, but I have ways to turn even the most pleasurable of events into something that resembles punishment. Isn't that right, my dear?"

Blythe's eyes widened. "Yes, Master." Her captor knew his way around punishment, and even on a good day his sadistic mind and methods could turn her into a compliant submissive.

"Let's proceed. I believe my girl is ready for her *thorough* examination."

~

The Alien's Mark

Sometimes submission comes at the end of a leash....

Blythe Wainwright thought she had her life together. At twenty-eight, as an anthropologist studying other planets in the galaxy, she had become comfortable with the predictability of her life. However, that steady calm ended the day their ship crashed onto the shores of the coastal town of Endermere, on the Planet Pra'kir. Suddenly, her fate, and that of her four other shipmates, was in the hands--and at the mercy--of the Pra'kirians.

With no wife or children, Dr. Xan Breckett had been married to his career, climbing the ranks, becoming a respected member of the medical field. But he had aspirations for himself with no clear indication of how to attain them until the Council of Nine gave him one of the aliens that had crashed onto their shores from Terra. The red-haired beauty assigned to him might be the key to opening doors... doors he didn't know existed.

But until he attained his career goals he'd train his ward--and pet-- along with Ganza, the nurse, and his assistant, Billex. Blythe's biting had been a nuisance in detention, but Xan knew how to treat a human whose only form of communication seemed to be biting, like an animal. He'd cure her of the vile behavior (and others, as well) no matter what harsh methods it took.

Though she was a grown woman, Blythe found herself held captive as a ward and pet in a household reminiscent of Victorian Earth. Under the authority of a very large, stern Pra'kirian - and one who expected complete and abject obedience she feared she had little hope of mercy.

But if she obeyed her stern captor, could she find contentment - and perhaps even happiness?

SHE SURVIVED THE CRASH...
    THEY'LL MAKE HER WISH SHE HADN'T

Now Available!

CAPTIVES OF PRA'KIR, BOOK 5: HER MASTER'S HANDS

Captives of Pra'kir, Book 5

Her Master's Hands

By

Kate Richards

Excerpt:

"Are you comfortable?"

The voice came from in front of her somewhere, and she leaned forward, wanting to connect with something, someone solid. "I'm sorry?"

"You need not apologize, merely answer." An older man, she thought, from the gravelly tone. Perhaps someone who could give her information, if not free her or loosen her bonds.

"I...my arms ache, and I'm frightened." Much as she hated to admit any weakness, she saw no option. "I wish I could see where we travel." She stopped, waited, but for a long moment no response came, and she feared it would not.

"You were quite distraught," he finally said. "My instructions are to do nothing to upset you again for fear you might harm yourself. "

"Harm? I've never harmed myself in my life." Despite the shooting pains in her shoulders and elbows, she strained to think. "I might have eaten too much chocolate from time to time..."

"This is not about food." They took a turn and, in her awkward position, Lily slid onto the floor.

"Oh, ouch."

A quick stop, and she was lifted by her aching arm back to the seat. "Why do you keep doing these things to yourself? The doctors will be very displeased if you break another bone."

"I have no idea what you're talking about." The whine in her voice could be attributed to pain and humiliation, but somehow the knowledge didn't make her like it any less. "Why would I cause myself pain?" She received no answer, and moments passed while she braced her feet on the floor and tried not to tumble onto the flooring again.

Everyone said space caused time disorientation but she'd never found it to be true. Blindfold her, though, take away her sight, and she didn't know if she'd been riding along for a day or a week. Or whatever they called time on this planet. If they were so concerned about keeping her from harm, they might consider cutting off the blood flow to her

She tried to stretch her awareness through her body, looking for... what did a broken bone feel like, anyway? "What bone did I break?"

"Between the terrible condition in which you arrived, and your attempted escape, a better question might be what bone did you not break?"

That was not the same voice. This one was younger, deeper, and smoother. Like warm caramel over ice cream on a hot afternoon. She shivered. "You're not the guy who was driving me."

"No." A muttered curse followed this and a hand gripped her arm. Lily whimpered.

"What the hell was someone thinking sending you bound like this. Hold on." More cursing

How do I know he's cursing? For that matter, how do I know what they are saying? She searched her memory but found nothing from her

ejection after the crash until she awoke in her present mode of trans-
portation.

"This is going to hurt. But I am afraid you might lose an arm if I
don't release you now. Hand me the knife from my kit. Okay, little girl,
bend forward a bit." She complied, eager for feeling to return with
her rapidly numbing fingertips. "Don't move."

~

Her Master's Hands

Liliana's last memory is of the terrifying crash landing. She and her
shipmates tumbling and screaming, the ship breaking up...but
they'd survived. At least she had. And her new masters promised the
others had as well, even if she was not allowed to see them. Masters.
How could a scientist from Earth submit herself to the control of a
pair of aliens, no matter how much her body loved their touch and,
humiliatingly, their punishments. Those big, hard hands give
pleasure as quickly as pain.

Aman and Cain shared a goal of finding the answer to the disease
ravaging the Mekrons, yet another alien species. Not only for the
aliens' sake, but because their malady shows signs of crossing into
the local population. Aman is sure a botanical solution can be
found; Cain is not so positive, but perhaps their fosterling's Earth
science background can help. Once they have done their job and
conditioned her to life on Pra'kir. A more stubborn female might
never be found, nor a more enticing one. Can she ever be part of life
in Endermere...part of their life?

Now Available!

ALSO, CHECK OUT THE ZANDIAN MASTERS SERIES BY RENEE ROSE!

His Human Slave

COLLARED AND CAGED, HIS HUMAN SLAVE AWAITS HER TRAINING.

Zander, the alien warrior prince intent on recovering his planet, needs a mate. While he would never choose a human of his own accord, his physician's gene-matching program selected Lamira's DNA as the best possible match with his own. Now he must teach the beautiful slave to yield to his will, accept his discipline and learn to serve him as her one true master.

Lamira has hidden her claircognizance from the Ocretions, as aberrant traits in human slaves are punished by death. When she's bought by a Zandian prince for breeding and kept by his side at all times, she finds it increasingly harder to hide. His humiliating punishments and dominance awake a powerful lust in her, which he tracks with a monitoring device on her arousal rate. But when she begins to care for the huge, demanding alien, she must choose between preserving her own life and revealing her secret to save his.

His Human Prisoner

HE DIDN'T BELIEVE IN DESTINY--UNTIL HE MET HER.

When a beautiful human slave steals Rok's ship and leaves him stranded on an abandoned planet, he's furious. Discovering her sister is the mate to the prince of his species only makes him more determined to find her and punish her thoroughly for her crimes. Yet when he captures her, he finds her impossible to resist. Punishment becomes exquisite pleasure as he teaches her to submit.

Lily's attraction to the huge Zandian warrior unnerves her. She's never been moved by a male, nor interested in sex before, but Rok coaxes every bit of emotion out of her as he demands her complete surrender. But he intends to turn her over to the authorities, which will mean her certain death. She must find a way to escape the handsome alien before she loses her life--or worse--her heart.

Training His Human

"YOUR OBEDIENCE TRAINING BEGINS TODAY."

Seke has no interest in owning or training a slave. Not even Leora, the beautiful human who had captivated his thoughts and fantasies since her arrival on their pod. As the Zandian Master of Arms, he has a war to plan and new troops to train. He can't be tempted by the breathtaking human slave, who, according to Prince Zander, grows aroused by punishment. Yet he can't allow another male to bring her to heel either. Not his Leora.

In all her lifetime as a slave, Leora might have submitted in body, but never in mind. But the prince has given her to the huge, scarred warrior, Seke, for punishment and she finds he has unexpected ways of bending her to his will. Ways that leave her trembling and half-mad with desire. But her new master is unwilling to take a new mate, and she fears that once he deems her training complete, he will set her aside, leaving her heart in pieces.

$\sim$

His Human Rebel

CONSCRIPTED BY AN ALIEN ARMY, SHE PLOTS HER ESCAPE...

Cambry doesn't believe the aliens' propaganda for one minute. The Zandians may have saved her from one death, but they planned to send her to another. She bides her time, waiting for her chance to get away and find her brother, enslaved by a different species. The only thing she didn't count on was Lundric, the tempting Zandian warrior who, for some reason, decided she was his female.

Lundric knew the fierce little rebel Cambry belonged to him the moment he saw her toss that auburn hair in defiance. He knows she hasn't accepted him or the Zandian's cause, but he vows to win her, no matter what it takes. But when Cambry steals a ship and attempts to escape, even his harshest punishment may not restore the trust between them.

$\sim$

His Human Vessel

HE PURCHASED HER TO BEAR A CHILD...HE WILL ALSO OWN HER SUBMISSION.

Bayla's destiny had been set from the beginning. Her body would be used for sex and breeding. Nothing changed when the sexy Zandian doctor purchased her from the baby farm and brought her to his examination room.

Nothing. And *everything.*

Daneth has always lived in his head, letting science govern his thoughts and choices. Having Bayla in his lab shouldn't change that, but somehow the submissive human female gets under his skin. No matter how harshly he punishes her, she responds to his touch with passion, sparking a lust that threatens to distract him from his plans.

When Bayla learns Daneth has a weakness for her, she presses her advantage, but she has no desire to bear yet another child and have it taken from her arms. If only she could figure out how to stay with the dominant alien doctor but avoid the pregnancy...

ALSO, CHECK OUT THE HAND OF VENGEANCE

~Winner, Best Erotic Sci-Fi, The Romance Reviews Reader's Pick Awards~

ON HIS PLANET, WOMEN ARE PUNISHED WHEN THEY DISOBEY...

DR. LARA SIMMONS can handle difficult surgeries on the battlefield of a war-torn planet. She can even handle her capture by rebels who need her skills to save the life of an important figurehead. But she wasn't prepared for being stuck out in the wilderness with Blade Vengeance, the fierce tattooed rebel warrior with antiquated views of gender roles and corporal punishment. Dominant and unyielding, he doesn't hesitate to take her in hand when she disobeys his rules. Yet he also delivers pleasure--with a passion she's never before experienced.

BLADE FINDS the doctor from Earth sexy as hell, especially when she's giving him attitude, but once he delivers her safely to headquarters, he pulls back from her allure. Known for single-handedly starting the revolution and freeing many of his people, his life is one of hardship, slavery and war. Going soft on a woman isn't part of his plan, especially with the final strike of the revolution so close. But when he sends Lara back to Earth to keep her safe during the upcoming battle, he inadvertently delivers her into enemy hands. Can he find and save her from the revolution he caused?

A NOTE FROM THE AUTHOR

Thank you for reading *Her Alien Masters!* If you enjoyed it, please consider leaving a review. It makes a huge difference in keeping down marketing costs for indie authors. *If you're not on my newsletter list, please sign up!* You'll get free books, bonus scenes, discounts, and my thoughts on D/s in books and the bedroom.

You can sign up at http://owned.gr8.com.

ACKNOWLEDGMENTS

Thank you to Katherine Deane and Maren Smith for beta reads and thank you to Dinah McLeod for coming up with this series idea and inviting me to participate!

WANT FREE RENEE ROSE BOOKS?

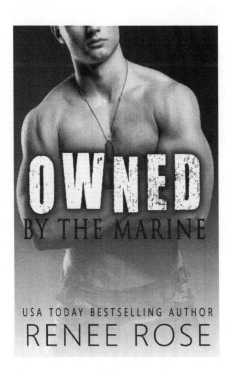

Go to http://owned.gr8.com to sign up for Renee Rose's newsletter and receive a free copy of *Owned by the Marine, Theirs to Punish, The Alpha's Punishment, Disobedience at the Dressmaker's* and *Her Billionaire Boss*. In addition to the free stories, you will also get special pricing, exclusive previews and news of new releases.

OTHER TITLES BY RENEE ROSE

Sci-Fi

The Hand of Vengeance, *His Human Slave*, *His Human Prisoner*, *Training His Human*, *His Human Rebel*, *Her Alien Masters* , *His Human Vessel (coming soon)*

Dark Mafia Romance

The Don's Daughter, *Mob Mistress*, *The Bossman*, *The Russian* (coming soon!)

Contemporary

Theirs to Protect, *Scoring with Santa*, *Owned by the Marine*, *Theirs to Punish*, *Punishing Portia*, *The Professor's Girl*, *Safe in his Arms*, *Saved*, *The Elusive "O" (FREE)*

Paranormal

The Alpha's Promise, *His Captive Mortal*, *The Alpha's Punishment*, *The Alpha's Hunger*, *Deathless Love*, *Deathless Discipline*, *The Winter Storm: An Ever After Chronicle*

Regency

The Darlington Incident, *Humbled*, *The Reddington Scandal*, *The Westerfield Affair*, *Pleasing the Colonel*

Western

His Little Lapis, *The Devil of Whiskey Row*, *The Outlaw's Bride*

Medieval

Mercenary, *Medieval Discipline*, *Lords and Ladies*, *The Knight's Prisoner*, *Betrothed*, *Held for Ransom*, *The Knight's Seduction*, *The Conquered Brides (5 book box set)*

Renaissance

Renaissance Discipline

Ageplay

Stepbrother's Rules, *Her Hollywood Daddy*, *His Little Lapis,*
Black Light: Valentine's Roulette (Broken)

BDSM under the name Darling Adams

Medical Play

Yes, Doctor, His Human Vessel (coming soon!)

Master/Slave

Punishing Portia, *His Human Slave*, *Training His Human*

ABOUT THE AUTHOR

USA TODAY BESTSELLING AUTHOR RENEE ROSE is a naughty wordsmith who writes kinky romance novels. Named Eroticon USA's Next Top Erotic Author in 2013, she has also won *The Romance Reviews* Best Historical Romance, and *Spanking Romance Reviews'* Best Historical, Best Erotic, Best Ageplay and favorite author. She's hit #1 on Amazon in the Erotic Paranormal, Western and Sci-fi categories. She also pens BDSM stories under the name Darling Adams.

Renee loves to connect with readers! Please visit her on:
   Blog: http://www.reneeroseromance.com/
   Twitter: https://twitter.com/ReneeRoseAuthor
   Facebook: https://www.facebook.com/reneeroseromance
   Goodreads:
http://www.goodreads.com/author/show/5895073.Renee_Rose
   Pinterest: http://pinterest.com/reneeroseauthor
   Instagram: http://instagram.com/reneeroseromance

96341878R00109

Made in the USA
Middletown, DE
30 October 2018